Emily Stuart Weed

Twilight Echoes

Emily Stuart Weed

Twilight Echoes

ISBN/EAN: 9783337248895

Printed in Europe, USA, Canada, Australia, Japan

Cover: Foto ©Andreas Hilbeck / pixelio.de

More available books at **www.hansebooks.com**

BY

EMILY STUART WEED

———

Life's music ever fails us
 Till its saddest strains are sung;
'Tis only out of sorrow
 That the sweetest notes are rung.

———

BUFFALO
CHARLES WELLS MOULTON
1890

BIGELOW PRESS: BUFFALO.

TABLE OF CONTENTS.

If I Sailed Away, ... 1

Come Back, ... 2

Till You Come, ... 3

Retrospect, ... 4

Christmas Chimes, ... 5

If We Only Knew, ... 6

Beyond the Sunset, ... 7

Yesterday — To-morrow, ... 8

Some One, ... 9

Good - night 10

For Aye, ... 11

How Strange, ... 12

All the Daylight, ... 13

Perhaps, ... 15

Shadows, ... 15

Promise, ... 17

The "Old Love," 17

Frost Kissed, ... 18

Dreams, ... 19

Erewhile, ... 21

Love's Return, ... 21

The Reaper, ... 22

Prescience, ... 23

Daffies, ... 24

Premonition, ... 25

Spring - Time, ... 26

iv

CONTENTS.

The Dead Year, ... 27
My Sailor, ... 28
Fidus Achates, ... 29
Greeting, ... 30
Sub Silentio, ... 30
Mine, ... , . . 31
The New Year, ... 32
Beautiful Hands, ... 33
Patience, ... 34
Maud, ... 35
Memory, ... 36
Life Colors, ... 38
April, ... 39
Promised, ... 40
Katydid, ... 41
Night, ... 42
Morté, ... 43
Aurora, ... 44
Charity, ... 44
My Dream, ... 45
Drifting Away, ... 46
I Wonder, ... 47
A Song of the Reapers, ... 48
Memories, ... 49
Under the Frost, ... 50
Unseen, ... 51
Beyond the Summer, ... 52
One Perfect Day, ... 53
Questioned, ... 54
My Twilight, ... 56
Lost, ... 57

Golden Harvest, ... 58
Autumn Blooms, ... 59
Returned, ... 60
To a Buttercup, ... 61
Ah! You Wonder, ... 62
Transmuted, ... 63
Glenville, ... 64
To ——, ... 65
"So Keep My Memory Green," 65
Pictures, ... 67
Melody, ... 68
A Message, ... 69
Heart Echoes, ... 69
When the Summer Dies, ... 70
Mile-Stones, ... 71
Reveries, ... 72
Heart-Ache, ... 73
May Blossoms, ... 74
When Do You Think of Me Most? 74
To the Picture of Longfellow's Children, . . . 75
Intuition, ... 76
Song of the Flowers, ... 76
Pilgrimage, ... 77
Unattained, ... 78
Incompleteness, ... 79
Sonnet, ... 80
Lines To G. H. C., ... 80
My Boat. 81
We Two, ... 82
Mrs. Browning, ... 83
Violets, ... 83

How? 84
Her Portrait, ... 85
Pond Lilies, ... 87
To ——, ... 88
A Christmas Greeting, ... 89
Her Room, ... 90
Indian Summer, ... 91
Seedlings, ... 92
Birthday Flowers, ... 93
To Mrs. ——, ... 93
Saint Valentine, ... 94
A Dream Recalled, ... 95
To C. C. H. at Sea, ... 96
Somebody Loves Me in Dreams, ... 97
"Three-Score and Ten," 98
Forever, ... 99
In Vain, ... 100
De Profundis, ... 101

SONG WORDS.

Drifting, ... 103
Answered, ... 104
Lullaby — Rest, ... 104
Bird and Wind, ... 105
Donald, ... 106
When the Year Grows Old, ... 106
Sailing, ... 107
My King, ... 108

OCEAN LETTERS.

To K. D., ... 109
To C. C. H., ... 111

Christmas Letter, ... 114
The Sleeping Beauty, ... 115
Capture of Stony Point by General Wayne, . . 121

POEMS FOR LITTLE ONES.

Little Elsie to the Flowers, ... 125
The Little Dauphin of France, ... 126
The Mouse and the Bee, ... 128
Jack's New Year, ... 131
Mischief, ... 133
The Lily Fairy, ... 135
The Spider and the Fly, ... 138
Pushed Out of the Nest, ... 142
Christmas Carol, ... 143

DRAMA FOR LITTLE ONES.

Love's Victory, ... 145

IMPROMPTU LINES.

To * * * 148
Omne Tempus, ... 148
Davis's Mill, ... 148
Thy Presence, ... 149
You, ... 149
St. Agnes Eve, ... 149
August Afternoon, ... 149
From Me to Thee, ... 150
Anon, ... 150

CHRISTMAS VERSES.

To ——, ... 151
To A. N., ... 151

To * * * 151
To ——, ... 152

AUTOGRAPH SCRAPS.

To S. M., ... 153
To A. M. W., ... 153
To C. S., ... 154
To Alice A., ... 154
To Louie W., ... 154
To C. H., ... 154
To L. R., ... 155
To H. E. S., ... 155
To N. S., ... 155
To F. S., ... 156

ACROSTICS.

Garfield, ... 157
Neal, ... 157
May, ... 157

BIRTHDAY VERSES.

To ——, ... 158
To C. C. H., ... 158

In Memoriam, ... 159

TWILIGHT ECHOES.

IF I SAILED AWAY.

What would you do, Dear Heart, if to-day
Over the seas I sailed away,
Out of sight of your earnest eyes,
Out of sound of your low replies,
Out of reach of your warm, white hand
That lies in mine, with a golden band,
Love's pledge that must bind us "forever and aye"—
But, what, Dear Heart, if I sailed away?

Whisper it low, and whisper it clear,
What would you do with all the year?
How would you meet the days and hours,
How could you visit our "Fern Land" and flowers?
Could you wander alone the daisied fields,
Or gather alone the " Autumn Shields "
Of gold and yellow, of crimson and gray,
If I sailed, Sweet Love, from your heart away?

Let your answer, mine own, be sweet and low.
Tell me, dear, you would miss me so
That life, and light, would darker be
If I sailed away on any sea.
For sail I must, Dear Heart, some day,
But my soul will claim you forever and aye.
Love can not die, though Time may cease—
Sweetheart, give, ere I sail, this peace.

COME BACK.

Ah, dear one, the sweet summer sunshine
  Still brightens the paths we have known,
And my heart still waits for your coming,
  Though the shadows have longer grown.

The moonlight that sleeps on the waters
  And silvered the crags by the sea,
Still shines over mountain and meadow,
  As it used, dear, for you and for me.

So come, ere my heart grows weary;
  The waiting has been so long;
Bring the melody back to my singing,
  The music into my song.

TILL YOU COME.

The nights are fair and sweet, love,
  And the morns, with fragrant dew,
But what are nights and mornings,
  Dear one, without you?

The fields are standing golden,
  The corn-flowers wave and bow,
They lean for me to pluck them,
  But how, dear, can I, how?

Without your eyes to look through,
  Without your helping hand,
The golden fields must tarnish,
  The corn-flowers longer stand.

My nights and all my mornings,
  However fair they be,
Can hold no touch of beauty,
  Till you come back to me.

RETROSPECT.

A dream, a vision of forest streams,
Of sunny days, of golden gleams,
Of wild-wood walks, of mossy glades
One sees in dreams in forest shades,
Comes o'er my soul like a west wind blown
Over fields of bloom with clover sown,

Comes over my heart this gladsome day,
While I count the hours as they throb away
Into the past, with the hours that died
When the summer waned into autumn-tide,
And left me to dream of the days to be,
Which only come back in dreams, to me.

The summer returned, but not as of old;
The sunsets showed more gray, less gold,
And the shadows cast from the steep hillside
Seemed a mantle made for the summers that died.
Ah! that they died, and only in dreams,
The sunny days, and the forest streams
Sweep over my heart like a west wind blown
Over fields of bloom with clover sown.

CHRISTMAS CHIMES.

The meadows are brown, the hills are all bare,
And up through the valley the clear, crisp air
  Is singing a Christmas song;
Like the song of the sea in the purple shell,
If we list to its notes it will sweetly tell
  The secrets it kept so long.

It tells of a time so sunny and fair,
When we watched the clouds of the snowy air
  For the reindeer's tiny form,
And saw in our dreams such pictures of light,
As we slept through the hours of the long dark night—
  Away from the clouds and storm.

Such pictures as glow in fairy tales,
When told at the hour when daylight pales,
  And the crimson west grows gray,
When we list for the chimes of fairy-bells,
That are hung in the shades of haunted dells,
  And are rung by goblin and fay.

It rings on the heart a tearful change
Of a darkened time, so sad, so strange,
  When our dreams had lost their light;

It whispers and sings to the leafless trees
Our secrets, that sigh in every breeze,
 Till the day wears into the night.

Oh, Christmas chimes! ye are merry and sad,
Ye wound the heart, and ye make it glad,
 With the music your ringing makes:
And the merry heart that has dreamed so long
Takes up the thread of the broken song,
 And sings till it, quivering, breaks!

IF WE ONLY KNEW.

If we only knew the heart-aches,
 The struggles and the tears,
That follow like a phantom
 The wake of human years.

Could we have known the shadows,
 That would cloud life's little day,
Known the cruel thorns in ambush
 Along the weary way;

How our tired feet would linger
 In the flush of early light—
If we knew at early dawning
 What we learn so late at night!

But the daylight wanes so quickly,
  And the gloaming falls so fast,
We are left with naught but shadows,
  Flying backward with the Past.

So with weary hearts and aching,
  Reaching out our souls have cried,
"If we only knew at dawning
  What we learn at eventide!"

BEYOND THE SUNSET.

We can not know if, after death,
  Life's babble through the golden bars
Shall float its doubts to the Far Beyond,
  That lies so dim beyond the stars.

In the "After-Day," when our dreams are proved,
  Beyond the sunset's golden wall,
If all our dreams of after-life
  Are proved but shadows after all,

What dreary blank for all our love,
  So unfulfilled, so long to wait,
So like the Peri, doomed to droop,
  And trail its wings outside the gate!

TWILIGHT ECHOES.

What though our waiting patient be,
  If naught remains but shadows pale,
In the "Vast Beyond," from which no light
  Can pierce the Future's misty vail!

And yet at times there wanders near
  The portal of our discontent
A whisper to our dreams of doubt,
  A benediction sweetly sent

To teach us that our fairest dreams
  Of all that lies beyond the "River,"
Are but the faintest gleams of light
  That *trusting* souls shall know forever.

YESTERDAY — TO-MORROW.

YESTERDAY.

Aye! the days are long since you held my hand,
Long days that run their golden sand
In sorrow and silence, in heart-ache and pain,
For the face I looked for so long in vain,
Long days, and weary, without the light,
That fashioned to morning my darkest night.

What broke our dream? Must I blame you, dear,
For the shadow that fell on love, so near?
We drifted apart, and the waves unkind
Left no track nor trace of our love behind,
Till the winds blew low, and the tide came back,
And "We Two" clasped hands from the wasteless track.

TO-MORROW.

With a blank marked out we'll begin anew:
Just love me, dear, as you used to do:
Watch for my coming and wish me a-near;
Dream of *my* face when you do dream, dear:
And over the Past, with its pain and sorrow,
We'll cast the joy of a glad To-morrow.

SOME ONE.

Never a wind that blows,
  E'en from the soft southwest,
But blows across the grave
  Of Some One we've loved best.

Some one sleeping too far
  Below the sweet sunshine
To hear the zephyr's breath
  As it stirs the myrtle vine,

Too far to know the footsteps
　　That softly, sadly pass
Above that quiet sleeping,
　　Below the tangled grass.

Some one, whose sandaled feet
　　Grew tired by the way,
Grew weary of the night,
　　And went forth to meet the day.

Oh, wild and wayward wind!
　　Oh, fragrant, soft southwest!
Ye kiss fair graves, in your roving,
　　Of a Some One we've *all* loved best.

GOOD-NIGHT.

Dear one, when I have said my last good-night,
　　If, stooping low to catch my latest breath,
Thy fondest heart shall lose the flickering light
　　I yield unto the shadowy boatman, Death,

Will morning break all strangely pale for thee,
　　And shadows hide thy heart away from dawn,
Because a presence loved has ceased to be,
　　Because a something out of life has gone?

Thy loving words came burdened thus, and fell
  Close to my heart, as dew on summer eves
Falls gently on the flowers it loves so well,
  At sunset hour, upon the drooping leaves.

Mine own, and if the sun shall coldly shine
  On days that may no longer light my place,
My *soul* shall wait for thee and know thee *mine*,
  Though years may hide me from my darling's face.

FOR AYE.

How will the roses know to bloom without thee,
  Thou who dids't mark their coming with thy light?
How will the lilies know to wake without thee
  Near to caress them as they turn from night?

The empty days draw out their weary length,
  And to their thresholds slowly wear away;
The moments pale and shiver as they go
  Slow through the windows of the weary day.

All through the amber hours the maple, sighing,
  Whispers and moans among the leafless trees
For one beneath its lengthened shadows lying,
  No more to glean among the golden sheaves.

One pulse in nature hushed, and silent, all;
  One heart-throb stilled, and mute the surging throng,
One chord but rudely swept, and moans the strain:
  One note in melody, and mute for aye, the song.

HOW STRANGE!

And this is life, ah, me!
So soon to lose the pearly light of dawn,
To find ere noon our fairest flowers gone
    From life! Ah, me!
Our light and flowers gone!

So strange, so sad, to miss
The blooming of the summer's first pale rose,
To lose the lily's sweetness as it blows
    Its perfumed kiss
To hearts its sweetness knows!

To wander on the hills
At early morn in search of something fair,
And find at eve'n naught but dead leaves there
    By sleeping rills
To twine among the hair,

Or on the heart to lie
In loving silence and in fragrance pressed,
Close to the loving heart and throbbing breast,
And there to die,
And, dying there, to rest!

Naught but dead locks!
No clustered violets fair along the stream
Where the pale wind-flowers doze and nod and dream,
And the lily rocks
All day upon the stream!

Ah, me! 'Tis strange! 'Tis sad!
To watch the rosy hues of life depart,
Behind the purple hills that stand apart,
From light we've had
Once on the aching heart.

ALL THE DAYLIGHT.

In this little dream and babble
    Mortals call the life of man,
Lose no time, but quickly gather
    All the daylight that you can.

For amid the hours of sunshine
  There are rays that all must lose:
So before the shadows lower
  Catch the nearest brilliant hues.

You will need them as you waken
  To the babble and the strife:
You will need them at the closing
  Of the last, long sleep of life.

When your eyelids grow too heavy
  For the day-beams to upraise,
If you've carried any brightness
  From the light of vanished days,

It will lead you through the shadows
  Each alone must surely tread,
And reflected tint the flowers
  Growing at the foot and head

Of the little mound that covers
  All that made the daylight fair
To the hearts that vainly sought it,
  Till *you* told them it was there.

PERHAPS.

'T was only a shadow, my heart said,
　As the sunlight fled away;
'T was only a shadow, and yet that shade
　Darkened all my day.

I watched so long for the daylight,
　And waited in vain for the dawn,
And I wept so long and bitterly
　When I found my light had gone!

Perhaps somewhere in the shadow,
　If I wait till it break o'er the lea,
I shall find, though it be in the gloaming,
　That my light is shining for me.

———

SHADOWS.

In the track of every sunbeam
　Lies a shadow that will hide
All the flowers it kissed at dawning
　In the shade of eventide.

Where the roses bloom at matin,
  Smiling by the lone wayside,
Showers of petals, found at vesper,
  Show us where the shadows hide.

Not the flowers so shadow-hidden,
  Breathing out the sweets of light,
Know alone the shade that follows
  Wearied hearts across the night,

Far across the starless silence,
  Breaking into empty day,
Bearing from our lives forever
  All the sunlight, far away;

Hiding from us all our treasures,
  In the darkness of the years,
Where it dashed the happy sunshine
  With a flood of blinding tears.

And our wearied hearts grow silent,
  And our poor lips too mute for speech,
As one by one our idols vanish,
  Or swiftly fly beyond our reach.

PROMISE.

Oh, grieve not that June-time and roses have vanished,
  And the soft airs of summer grown heavy and chill,
Nor that green on the hillside for brown has been ban-
    ished,
  For a summer lies hid that the frosts can not kill.

And as sure as the sunlight that now coldly glances,
  And stirs not a throb in the heart, sleeping low,
Will it fall in caresses, and waken sweet fancies,
  For the summer *must* come, and the roses *will* blow.

Then despair not, though slowly her eyelids shall open
  In the dreamland of flowers, her waking be late,
For the sweet summer-time with her blossoming token
  Will surely return to the heart that can wait.

THE "OLD LOVE."

Into the heart of the golden summer,
  Unfolded to the year,
Into the soul of its throbbing bosom,
  Gilding its far and near,

Has drifted the light of a golden glory,
  Fairer than light of day,
That will live long after the summer's gone,
  The summer that will not stay.

And the days to come in the summers to be
  Will glow with the love-light left them,
Ere the soul of the year had burned so low,
  In the altar-fires that bereft them.

The self-same light will find its way
  To the heart of the wayside places,
And the old love look out the same
  From all the wayside faces.

FROST-KISSED.

How chill the phantom breath of autumn
  Sweeps o'er the green of Nature's face,
Turning to brown the hillside beauty,
  With dead leaves left to mark the place!

Slowly and sadly they droop and fall,
  No sigh of blight, nor secret pain,
As they are falling, silently falling,
  Never to rise from the earth again.

The days grow sad and fall as the leaves,
  With the weight of sorrow to make them fall.
And a cry goes up that ever is heard
  For the days that never come back at a call.

Fall, many-hued and brilliant leaves,
  And sunny days with sorrow worn;
Heart-break and frost-kiss are ever the same,
  Though born of June or October morn.

Ever the same blight rests on each,
  Whether the heart of a leaf or a mortal;
It banishes hope and slays for aye
  The seraph of life that lighted its portal.

DREAMS.

TO C. C. H.

I have been thinking to-day, dear,
  Or perhaps I dreamed it so,
As I watched the sun go out of the west,
  Watched, till he sank so low,

That the crimson and gold grew purple,
  And the purple faded to gray,
As I sat in the shadows that softly fell
  With the twilight that covered the day.

And thought, or dreamed, it may be,
　Of a beautiful day in June,
When the roses were blowing their sweetness out,
　And life seemed all a-tune

With its fragrance, and joy, and sunshine,
　And the notes of a low, sweet rhyme,
That was sung to me, dear, by lips not strange,
　In that lost sweet "summer time."

I may look in the Junes to come,
　In the summers yet to be,
But the light, and the music, and sweetness gone
　Will never drift back to me.

And the dream of to-day in the sunset
　Was only a dream of the past,
I reached for the sunlight, dear, but found
　Only the shadow it cast.

．　　　　　．　　　　．　　　．　　．

If One shall break our idols, dear,
　To whom we mutely pray,
'Tis that our hearts may learn to serve
　The Master, not the clay.

EREWHILE.

Your dreams must lose their light,
  And the darkness bide awhile,
And the music go out of the song,
  Ere your lips may learn to smile.

The roses must bloom and fade,
  The blossoms lie dead at your feet:
The bud be crushed in your hand
  Ere its heart will shed the sweet.

Aye! Dreams, and roses, and life
  Must know some shadow of night,
And the heart bow low in the dust,
  Ere beauty and fragrance and light.

LOVE'S RETURN.

Love flew by one sunny day,
  Heard the call within my heart,
Straightway turned and entered in,
  Vowing never to depart.

All the day he touched to splendor,
  All the hours to music set;
Soon my heart caught up the singing,
  Echoed: "Love can ne'er forget."

But, alas! the days grew shadowed,
  Love proved truant to his trust,
Spread his wings and lightly vanished,
  Left my spirit in the dust.

All the days seemed turned to sorrow,
  Till again Love kissed my face,
Came repentant, loved and claimed me,
  Smiling with a threefold grace.

THE REAPER.

He came in the watches of midnight,
  When the eyelids were folded down,
And lifted the sable curtain,
  To proffer the golden crown
To him who had soonest grown weary
  Among the tired train
Of gleaners, whose arms had wearied,
  Gathering the scattered grain.

He passed the couch of manhood,
  Nor wakened youth's deep dream,
But still searched on for the weariest
  By the light of the golden gleam,
Till it fell on the brow of childhood,
  More tired than all the rest,
In the cot of a little sleeper,
  Then paused by the throbbing breast

That told who had soonest grown weary
  In the life-race scarce begun;
Told who of the gleaners had fainted,
  Leaving the task undone,
And the Reaper stooped low with the jewel
  He had brought for the brow most fair,
And placed it in the keeping
  Of the weariest gleaner there.

PRESCIENCE.

Where do the flowers stay,
  All the rare blooms of the year?
Cans't tell me, where are they,
Spring buds and blossoms gay,
  Whose coming seems a-near?

Mystery of daffodil,
  Crocus and violet fair
Shadows the barren hill,
Lingers beside the rill,
  Lives in the balmy air.

Slumbering truants, I wis,
  Dainty with purple and gold,
Lie waiting the soft spring kiss,
And the sunshine they must miss,
  Under the darksome mold.

DAFFIES.

I send you some Daffies this morning,
  My earliest spring surprise;
They will tell you of April sunshine,
  With a breath of April skies.

They slept through the storms of winter,
  And dozed through the March wind's song,
When the April sunshine waked them
  With the *first* of the flower-throng.

So I send them to bear you a greeting,
  With the first the flowers may bring
Of fragrance, and beauty, and sunshine,
  My "cuckoo song" of the spring.

PREMONITION.

You will know, dear, when I lie a-dying,
  Though no word should mind you as I go
      Into the silent Land.
The wind's low music will be hushed to sighing,
  And all life's joyous notes to minor flow,
      As ebbs life's sand.

Out of the vast and careless multitude,
  One heart will miss the echo of its own,
      And listen for its throbbing,
Finding but silence in the interlude,
  No answer but the weary undertone
      Of nature sobbing.

Though no word be spoken, you will know, dear,
  Across the silence I will send the sign
      Of life's broken dream.
As fall the darkness and the shadows drear
  Across the silent night, to you will shine
      Life's parting beam.

Only an atom of God's infinite made nante,
  Yet all for love of it some heart will ache,
      Some soul make moan.
And so, dear, where is hushed life's trembling lute,
  I shall not fear the sleep from which none wake,
      Under the stone.

SPRING-TIME.

The fair young Spring is here,
  Just waking from the Winter's snowy drifts,
    And slyly looking up;
Out of the frozen mere,
  Out of the winter dream of bloomy rifts,
    Will wake some fairy cup.

Some tiny flower bell,
  Pushing its dainty head to catch the light,
    Above the darksome mold
Will softly, sweetly tell
  The Spring-time near and woo the sunshine bright,
    Its beauty to unfold

Some star-eyed flowret, pale
  From sleeping long amid the mosses sere,
    Will waken with a blush,
Kissed by the roving gale
  That stoops him low to dry the dew-drop tear
    Distilled mid nature's hush.

THE DEAD YEAR.

The dead year lies with folded hands
    And silent, upturned face;
Emptied the glass of its golden sands,
Empty, and idle, and lone it stands.
    Alas! for the tender grace!
Alas! for the broken bands!

Wrapped in a robe of snow he lies;
    We may not break his sleep.
His ear is dulled to our tenderest cries!
As ever the same when a true heart dies;
    The old year slumbers deep,
The dead year ne'er will rise.

Gone to sleep with the buried years
    That hide in the misty past,
The old year sleeps despite our tears;
The dead year lies without our fears,
    The year that would not last
Despite our warmest tears.

MY SAILOR.

How could I know my sailor had lain
　Fathoms deep in the ocean blue?
　　How could I guess he had slept so long,
　　Lulled by the notes of the sea's low song?
On the coral bed of the ocean plain,
How could I know of my sailor slain?

I had watched each day till the sun's low beams
　Touched to gold the snowy sail,
　　As each came up from the under world
　　With prow high set, and sheets unfurled,
Up from the sea, bringing golden dreams,
Fair as the sunset's painted gleams.

Out on the beach, I learned it late,
　Alone by the waves, in the moonlight pale,
　　The ceaseless surge that washed the shore,
　　Sang of the days that could come no more,
Bringing golden dreams and a fairer freight,
And my heart for its sailor forever must wait.

FIDUS ACHATES.

What gift from the mist and shadow,
  In the hurry and bustle of life,
Do we reach for and long for most,
  Out of the dust and strife?
Out of the coming and going,
  Amid the losses and gains,
What do we ask as a recompense
  For a harvest of tears and pains?

Only a hand to lead us
  Over the thorny way,
Some patient heart to whisper
  When our feet shall go astray:
Only a rest, by the wayside,
  When we've grown aweary of tears,
A tenderness gleaned from the harvest of love,
  Best gift for our toilsome years.

GREETING.

Sweet heart, a kiss from the spring,
In buds the March winds bring,
A kiss with the promise of days to be,
A song of the summer for you and me,
As sung by bird, and blossom, and bee,
    And scent of the sweet red clover.

A song of the hidden June,
When its world is all a-tune,
Lies in the heart of the folded leaf,
A promise of harvest and golden sheaf,
In buds that sleep for a season brief,
    Till the March King's reign is over.

SUB SILENTIO.

If I lose my way and wander far
From the sound of the music and dancing feet,
You will find me alone in a quiet nook,
With closed lids hiding a tired look,
    In a dream 'mid blossoming clover.

Tired of the dancing, and very tired
Of the song with the music all gone out.
You will find me alone in a starless night,
With a dream of *you*—the only light
    When the other dream is over.

You will know me by signs that the silence will give,
In the fold of gown and clasp of hand,
With a white rose frozen in finger tips,
With the trace of dead kisses long laid on dead lips.
    Hid away 'neath the blossoming clover.

MINE.

The Summer is ended, but not the song
    That the Summer hours sang low to me;
It will float through the hours of the faded year,
    Till the Summer and song come back to me.

I shall hear it all through the storm and shine
    Of the Autumn days, that will hide your face
In the Winter winds, that will sing to the hills
    The self-same song with a Summer grace,

And carry it down to meet the Spring,
  Whose fragrant breath from beyond the sea
Shall kiss to life the Summer that died
  With the song on its lips that it sang for me.

THE NEW YEAR.

The New Year stands at the door,
  With holly branch and bough;
    Crowned with smiles he stands,
    Filled with gifts his hands;
  He wears no clouded brow
For the year that is no more.

Greet him with smiles as true
  As he brings in the breaking dawn;
    Outshining the morning stars,
    He beams through golden bars,
  And low! the night is gone,
The New Year greeteth you!

BEAUTIFUL HANDS.

Beautiful hands are not always white,
  Shapely and fair to see,
But are often cast in an humble mold,
  And are brown as brown can be.

Useful hands, that are ready to take
  Life's duties, one by one;
Hands that are willing to reap and glean
  Till the reaper's work be done,

Lifting the burdens we find so hard
  To bear through life's long day,
Brushing the dead leaves, sorrow drops
    From out life's tangled way.

Gentle hands, between whose palms
  The weary face may lie;
Beautiful hands, that softly tell
  For sorrow the reason why.

Hands whose touch remains for years,
  Dear hands, though folded low,
Whose magic thrills within our souls,
  Whispering, "We loved you so."

Warm human hands that once we held
  So close within our own;
Though now clasped cold, their silent clay
  Still speaks in love's low tone,

Telling the weary heart the song
  It learned in years gone by:
Beautiful hands are always found
  Where the heaviest duties lie!

PATIENCE.

Just because 't is Winter, dear,
  And no flowers are seen,
Don't forget the snow-drifts hide
  Germs of Summer green.

Waiting for the Spring to come,
  Folded leaf and flower
Patiently abide the time
  Of the opening hour.

Waiting for the storms to pass,
  Waiting for the sun

To unfold the tiny leaves,
　　Slowly, one by one.

Just because you're tired, dear,
　　And the night seems long,
Don't forget the morning dawns
　　With a restful song.

Just beyond the sunset's gold,
　　Where no snows are seen,
You will find the whole year's buds
　　In a Summer green.

Look beyond the Winter drifts,
　　You will find the Spring;
Look through nature's storm and shine
　　Up to Nature's King.

———————

MAUD.

The name that is cut in this marble cold
Is only the trace of a tale that is told,
　　　A silent history,
　　　　Hiding its own
　　　Strange life mystery
　　　　Under the stone.

Only "Maud" in the marble white,
"Our only one," no other light,
  Carved with the years
   On the silent stone,
  To tell of tears,
   Or echo a moan.

Under the stars that watch her sleep,
Far from life's babble, still and deep,
  She rests with the night
   And makes no moan,
  'Neath the column white
   Of the sculptured stone.

We only know, as we softly pass
Through the tangled mesh of the drooping grass,
  Of a fair young life
   That went out alone,
  Leaving the strife
   To sleep 'neath the stone.

MEMORY.

There's a painter whose years are unnumbered,
 Whose talents are strange as his name,
And he frescoes many a dwelling
 With pictures of ancient fame.

TWILIGHT ECHOES.

He visits the walls of the kingly,
  He dwells in the peasant's dream,
He colors his picture with fancy,
  And tints with a golden beam.

Sometimes in his mood they are darker,
  And often are covered with tears
That he sheds like a mist o'er the picture,
  To mantle the buried years.

Sometimes he brings sketches of childhood,
  Where laughter is blended with cries,
And his pictures of youth and its pleasures
  Are formed on a canvas of sighs.

He never grows weary of labor,
  Nor tires of his visits to man,
Though he labors through wearisome ages
  And traverses years at a span.

He calls not for title nor honor,
  Nor envies the scroll of Fame,
But renown unbidden attends him,
  For "Memory" is his name.

LIFE COLORS.

It will never be what you dream, dear,
　Take my word, the colors will fade;
The picture you've painted all sunshine
　Must be touched and re-touched with shade.

You will sigh that so often the crimson
　Must be flecked here and there with the gray,
But the morning, the noon and the evening
　Must be used to complete the full day.

You are painting a picture of life, dear,
　Where sunshine and clouds must abide,
And the shadows that come not at dawning
　Must fall with the dim eventide.

Where those roses grow fair from the hedges
　Paint some thorns—make the picture complete;
The bloom that the fingers may gather
　You will learn hides thorns for the feet.

The gold that shines out from the sunset
　Must be tarnished by purple and gray,
Ere the curtain of night is unfolded,
　Shutting out all that's left of the day.

But, dear, when you've ended the dreaming,
  And life's weary pilgrimage made,
You'll find it the picture you dreamed of,
  In colors that never will fade.

APRIL.

Crocus buds of white and gold,
Shyly peeping through the mold,
Now their beauty all unfold,
    Born of the April weather.

Where hid they so long in the dark,
Out of sight in garden and park,
Not a sign their bed to mark,
    Now blowing all together?

April showers kissed them sleeping,
April breezes dried their weeping,
April sunshine caught them peeping
    From the darksome nether.

PROMISED.

Athwart the chill November sky
　The leaden clouds hang dull and low,
The pulseless air gives forth no sign
　Across the stubble brown with woe.

The withered leaves in crumpled heaps
　Lie brown and dead on upland moor,
And through the valley nature weeps
　Her life-blood tears on all she bore.

High on the birchen tree-top swings
　The blue-bird's nest and summer home,
Rocked no more by the soft south wind,
　Sheltered by naught but the pale blue dome.

Blue-bird, and jay, and oriole fair
　Have flown to the cuckoo's warm retreat,
And under sunny southern skies
　Their northern songs will soon repeat.

Birch, and beach, and linden boughs
　Waived them adieu with many sighs;
All lonely the oak in his sturdy grace
　Joined with the leafless forest cries.

But the south wind whispers of sunny hours,
And a secret tells to the northern plain
Of a day not distant, when smiling Spring
Shall return with the cuckoo's joyous strain.

KATYDID.

Katydid, Katydid, how can you sing?
Sing the long night through, making it ring.
Ring forth the cadence on hours that are flying,
"The Harvest is over, the Summer is dying."

Long has she lingered in valley and plain,
Long have we loved her, but wooed her in vain.
Soon will she fly us, and naught of our crying
Can call back the hours of the Summer that's dying.

Katydid, Katydid, sing while you may,
Sing while the night lasts, sing and be gay,
Chant your own requiem, stop not for sighing,
The Summer is fading, and soon you'll be dying.

Dying alone as the leaves droop and leave you;
Dying at night, the pale stars will grieve you;
Gazing so pitiless, while you are crying
"My Harvest is over, and now I am dying."

NIGHT.

The golden West had changed its hues,
  And amber faded into gray:
The purple shadows fell like mist,
  And, lingering, hid the light of day.

The dewy twilight kissed the hills,
  And wrapped the daisies in a dream;
The pale young moon peeped shyly forth,
  And tipped the groves in silvery sheen.

The katydid piped shrill and clear,
  The cricket sang his song of mirth,
The breeze had lulled the birds to rest,
  And night fell softly on the earth.

Fair night, with all its silent hours
  Lighted with lamps from her starry dome,
Bathing the lone and silent hills,
  Kissing the cot and the palace home.

Falling alike on the happy and sad,
  Dropping her mantle to cover earth's breast,
Wrapping the soul in her folds of peace,
  Night lulls the weary ones sweetly to rest.

MORTÉ.

Oh, happy sleep that knows no waking!
  Oh, happy dream that knows no pain!
Stoop low and fold us in thy keeping:
  Stoop low, sweet dream, with sweet refrain.

Fold down upon the wearied heart
  The peace that follows after sleeping;
Stoop low and dry the tears that start
  From eyes that once knew naught of weeping.

Kiss dry the moistened, troubled cheek,
  Oh, happy, restful, blessed dream,
Clasp mute the weary hands and meek
  With life's last weary fading beam.

Far through the hours of the fair young year
  And through the summer's changeful bloom,
Into the autumn brown and sere,
  We watch and wait for sleep to come.

And far adown the purple west
  Our sun sinks slowly out of sight,
And far adown the earth we rest,
  In sleep and dreams of restful night.

AURORA.

Morn breaks in beauty from the curtained night,
   And throws her kisses back,
And sends her silvery smiles of light
   Along the eastern track.

The pale stars hide in creeping mist,
   And the fair young crescent fades:
Fainter the twinkling train appears,
   As fly the ebon shades.

Across the threshold of the night
   The golden glory falls;
Aurora kisses all the hills
   With rosy shimmering calls.

CHARITY.

Live not for self, but strive for others' good,
   And if life's rue is dealt with hand unsparing,
Put not the cup in haste, or wrath, away,
   Nor droop beneath the cross that thou art bearing.

If for another's woe thy heart shall ache,
  One notes thy grief and marks the record true;
And every tear that's wept for other's sake
  Is garnered to distill in heavenly dew.

Life's darkened hours may find some ray of light
  To shed upon the sorrowing hearts that share them,
If we but bear each other's burdens well,
  And lift the clouds of grief from souls that wear them.

Let sunshine in; give all that thou cans't spare;
  And all thy bread upon the waters cast
Will come again with life's returning billows,
  Laden with blessings from out the clouded Past.

MY DREAM.

Last night I dreamed of a fairy lake,
  And a boat by fairies made,
And I cried to follow the silvery track
  The fairy boat had made.

The bark was moored the long bright day,
  Till the sun went down in the west;
The south wind bore me the word "*Farewell*,"
  Shrouding my heart with unrest.

A vision went out through the twilight mist
  With a "boatman pale" in the bark;
My life-light went the self-same way
  And was lost in an echoless dark.

DRIFTING AWAY.

We are drifting away on the stream of life,
  Far from the shore of our childhood's time;
We are leaving the banks of our sunny youth
  For an unknown port and a foreign clime.

We've launched our bark on the drifting tide,
  That is bearing us out to the open sea;
We can never return to those shores of youth,
  That echo the songs of our childish glee.

We can only look back at the fading shore,
  Only dream over the happy past,
Yet memory will keep the pictured dream
  Though the shadow of years o'er the dream is cast.

And when we are tossed on the troublous tide
  By the pitiless waves, unseen and alone,
When our cry for help is caught by the winds
  And echoed again by the sea's low moan,

Faint not, though the night be long and dark:
  There's a calm that will visit the ocean's breast:
And the gleam of light from our vanished years
  Shall beacon the care-worn and weary to rest.

I WONDER.

I wonder if I shall be missed,
    I wonder if any will grieve,
When my task is ended, my mission done,
When the circle is broken, and only one
    In life's woof shall have ceased to weave?

I wonder if days will seem longer,
    If nights in their darkness more drear,
When my voice is hushed, my mirth is stilled,
When the rooms echo silence, that ever were filled
    With sounds of my gladness and cheer?

I wonder, and wonder, and wonder,
    Till wondering wearies my brain,
To know if the hearts that could love me here,
Would love me when silent, and shed one tear,
    And if weeping would bring them pain?

Alas for the hearts that shall mourn us!
Alas for the tears of weeping!
Ah, me! for the hearts that shall mutely pray
Beside their loved ones, hid from day,
In dreams of an endless sleeping!

A SONG OF THE REAPERS.

The summer is ended, the harvest is o'er
And the Reapers are merrily singing
Under autumn-flecked banners of russet and gold,
Waving over the treasures they're bringing.

What bring they, these Reapers, you ask as they sing,
Through the autumn fields dressed in their glory?
Go question the Summer that hid in her heart
A song of "The old, old story."

Go learn from the Summer that died in the lap
Of the Autumn days waiting to crown her,
The song that she sang of treasures untold
To be found when the days grew browner.

Days crowned at last with the gold they held,
Hearts joined that naught could dissever,
Hands clasped with a faith in the days to be,
Of a love that would last forever.

Aye, gleaners of hearts, these Reapers that tell
  Of the harvest of gold they are bringing,
A song rings out o'er the fields they've gleaned,
  And *Love* is the song they're singing.

MEMORIES.

Only a memory of buried years,
  Only a dream that could not last,
Only a thought, and yet these tears,
  Tears that will flow till the dream be past.

Ah, me! the wonder of life's sad dream,
  There all must wake to endure and die,
There all must learn of sorrow's sway
  And never may know the reason why!

Till we hear in the hush of a new-born day
  The "low, sweet song" that the seraphs sing,
Beyond the night, where our darlings wait,
  Our hearts shall know before the King.

UNDER THE FROST.

I mourn for the loss of my beautiful May,
  And June with her roses fair;
I call in vain for the violets pale
  That scented the morning air.

The harebell and the lily, too,
  Have drooped their beautiful heads,
And the pink and the perfumed mignonette
  Are hid in their frosty beds.

The aster and the sunflower,
  That stood by the garden wall,
Have gone with the breath of the roses
  To answer the frost-king's call.

And the crimson and gold of the maple
  Have changed to a russet brown,
Since the icy sweep of the frost-king
  Through the heart of the drowsy town.

It caught the flowers while napping,
  And bound them with a spell;
It left them mute on the hillside
  And lifeless in the dell.

They have gone to sleep, and the fairies
　Will revel till summer showers
Shall bring me back my roses,
　And beautiful truant flowers.

———————

UNSEEN.

The shadow falls across the hearth
　We thought no cloud could darken:
Our loved ones vanish in the shade
　The while we would not hearken.

Our hearts so loudly beat their love
　For those to whom we're clinging,
We do not hear the whispered call,
　Nor heed the choral singing.

We sing our quiet sabbaths, down
　Close to the kirk-yard kneeling:
We only hear the solemn tones
　From the holy organ pealing.

So close the shadow folds its wing,
　Beside our loved ones praying,
Our eyes are dimmed, we only feel
　The shadow in its staying.

Till, reaching for the loved one's hand
  That warmly clasped our own,
We find but mute, unanswering clay,
  No echo but our moan!

BEYOND THE SUMMER.

I could not speak with your face so near,
  Though I knew the summer days would sleep.
My words would form, and falter, and fall
  Unspoken, because my heart would weep.

Do you think in the days that drifted by,
  With only the music your singing wrought,
That I loved you less, though the songs were few.
  When love was the song your singing brought?

Your every gift I keep in sight;
  Their treasured sweetness mutely tells
Of a love that was *mine, mine only*, dear,
  Till I missed the music of "Fairy Bells."

Life's path is short! Love's way is long!
  'Twill live beyond the summer days,
When our lips are still, our hands are clasped.
  And our tired feet have learned other ways.

ONE PERFECT DAY.

So fair, so very fair,
That one sweet perfect day.
So fair, that never day on earth
Can come again with so much light
As came that one fair sunny day with thee.
Each little flowret smiled,
And every forest leaf
Gave back through hazy autumn mists
The look of love that, smiling, smiled on me.

The far-off hills seemed near,
So near to me that day,
That every whispered word would seem
To nestle in their far-off depths,
To come to me again singing of thee.
Their silent purple shade
Grew light with look of thine,
That wandered to the woodland's brow,
And, smiling, kissed the flowers upon the lea.

The maple's golden boughs
Swung low to touch thy cheek,
As passing near their scarlet lips
They fain would drop upon thine own,
One pledge of faith in all thy loveliness.

The river, slowly winding
Through the autumn's blaze
Of shining gold and purple bloom,
Reflected with a smile thy perfect fairness.

Oh, more than perfect day!
That came with thee, and went
Into my shadowed life and out,
As fades the pale and quiet light
Of far-off beams from out the evening star,
Leaving remembered light
Of loveliness and thee
To mind me of the perfect rays
That shine from "Heaven's forget-me-nots" afar.

QUESTIONED.

Daisies, did ye listen
Last night to hear me pass,
Brushing the bloom from the clover,
The dew from the dripping grass?

The bee had hid from the moonlight,
And lay in the clover cup,
And, daisies ye seemed to be sleeping,
For your petals were folded up!

And your pale sweet faces nodded
  Among the tangled grass,
But, daisies, tell me truly,
  Did ye list to hear me pass?

For Harold and I went lightly
  As shadows through the flowers,
As softly as the moonlight
  That kissed the sleeping hours.

But I heard it from the plover,
  That pipes in the meadow grass,
And the thrush sang loud from the hawthorn,
  "The daisies saw you pass,

And heard your promise to Harold,
  As he whispered under a breath,
To be constant, and tender, and loving,
  And faithful unto death!"

Oh, modest, meek-eyed daisies!
  Ye told that ye heard me pass,
Brushing the bloom from the clover,
  The dew from the dripping grass!

MY TWILIGHT.

I had not looked for the deepening
  Of shadows so soon in my sky;
I had not thought that the crimson
  So quickly would fade and die.

For my dreams had been so golden,
  As they cradled me through the night,
I sang, "Naught of shadow can darken
  A day that must dawn so bright."

But at waking my heart grew silent,
  Of the song that had filled it with glee,
The song that seemed born of the brightness,
  The melody waiting for me.

I had thought to walk where the roses
  Grew fairest without the thorn;
I had dreamed to find them at even
  As fair as I plucked them at morn.

But the shadows fell, hiding the flowers,
  And my feet strayed into the night,
While I gathered the thorns with the roses,
  In the misty and dim twilight.

TWILIGHT ECHOES.

My heart bowed low in the gloaming
 'Neath the mantle of twilight gray,
As the sunbeams I'd thought to garner
 With the crimson faded away.

LOST.

Oh! have you seen my baby fair,
With bright brown eyes and sunny hair,
 Roaming the meadow-lands—
A tiny form, with yellow hair
That stole the sunshine and held it there,
 Prisoned in golden bands?

There never was a fairer face;
You'll know it by a nameless grace
 In dainty baby ways;
With moistened ringlets out of place,
Blown about in a butterfly chase,—
 How long my darling stays!

Knee-deep in the clover and grasses sweet,
Where the violet blue and Mayflowers meet,
 I left my darling at play:

At noontide I left her away from the heat,
But I've lost the trace of her tiny feet,
   'Mid the grasses and flowers gay.

    *   *   *   *   *   *   *   *

Oh! pray you look on my baby fair,
With folded hands, and tarnished hair,
   And brown eyes hid from the light!
From the meadow lands she wandered where
The river sands lay white and bare;—
   Ah, me! how dark the night.

GOLDEN HARVEST.

Walk forth in the light of to-day,
   To-morrow may never dawn:
Scatter roses and smiles by the way,
   Bringing sheaves at eventide home.

Lift the drooping and weary ones up,
   Leave no tired heart to the night;
Press no bitterness into their cup,
   Bear them into the sunshine and light.

For your harvest will golden be,
  If you scatter the sunlight and flowers,
As the morn on the upland lea,
  As the sunshine after the showers.

AUTUMN BLOOMS.

The springtide woos from many vales
  The sweets so deeply hidden,
And flowers along life's wayside bloom
  For many hearts unbidden.

Kissed into life by summer showers,
  Their petals open wide;
Softly they breathe their fragrance out
  While summer hours abide.

But ere the coming of the frost,
  Sometimes the year forgets,
And autumn brings a feast of blooms
  The springtide ne'er begets.

        .   .   .   .

Expectant hearts oft miss the hour
  The roses have for blowing,
But find in Autumn sweeter buds
  Than come from springtide sowing.

RETURNED.

The spring is near: I know by the sound
　Of the soft wind through the trees;
I know by the scent of the meadow-lands
　That is borne on the morning breeze:
I know by the sound of the dancing brook
　As it leaps, and ripples, and sings,
And hurries along from the mountain-top
　With the moistening life it brings.

The distant hills so dim and far
　Seem near through the soft gray mist,
And the brown valleys tinged with green,
　And the plains that spring has kissed,
The purple heather and violet blue,
　Are peeping through mossy beds,
While the daffodil betrays her birth
　By the perfumed breath she sheds.

The chirp of the robin at eventide,
　The swallows' twitter at morn,
And tiny song of the humming-bee,
　Proclaim that spring is born.
The tinkling bells of the distant folds,
　The lowing of herds in the gloaming,
Ring out on the quiet evening air
　The music of spring's returning.

TO A BUTTERCUP.

Pale little flower plucked from the grasses,
  Hidden away in the daisies' shade,
Hold thy wee face up, list while I tell thee
  Why thou wast plucked, and why thou wast made.

Born for a mission, thy petals unfolded,
  Nurtured by sunlight and fed by the dew,
Kissed by the butterfly, watched by the clover,
  Never, oh! never a sweeter bud grew.

Called to the light, thy being was spoken,
  Thy daintiness culled for a casket of trust,
And the sweet of thy blowing must mix with the treasure
  I leave in thy heart till thy petals are dust.

I will write on thy leaves such a legend of love,
  As shall rival all tales of the "Old, old story";
I will sing to thy petals a song as sweet
  As the echoes might waft from the regions of glory.

Let the secret, "I love her," be hid in thy heart,
  And held in thy keeping through life's long day,
And whenever she looks on thy face, though faded,
  Sing to her softly the words I would say.

AH! YOU WONDER.

Ah! you wonder that I love you!
  All the gold of earth is mine.
In the light of tender glances
  Earth's dark spots with glory shine.

Else how could the sunlit hours
  With such golden beauty glow,
Or the river in its singing
  With such music sweetly flow?

How could every note of song-bird
  Seem a choral anthem sung
In among the greenwood branches,
  Had not love the changes rung?

How could I among the grasses
  Pluck the flowers His love has given,
Had their sweetness not reflected
  In your love so much of Heaven?

Ere you came my heart divined you,
  Love's low singing bade me wait,
Whispering, "Patience! One is coming
  Who will ope you Eden's gate."

TRANSMUTED.

What set the days to music?
　What made the daylight fair?
What waked my heart to singing
　Love's melody unaware?

The yesterdays lie hidden
　Behind the glad to-day;
The morrows seem to promise
　A love to last for aye.

The night is filled with shining
　Of stars unseen before;
New beauty gilds the morning,
　The shadows come no more.

Dear heart, you hold the magic
　That makes December May;
Your soul touched mine while sleeping,
　And turned the night to day!

GLENVILLE..

Do you remember, dear,
  That day we walked together
Atween the hedges set with gold,
  And blooms like purple heather?

Along the winding road
  That hid in many a hollow,
And ankle-deep in ferny beds
  Our steps were wont to follow?

And through the sweet excess
  The meadow-lands were rich in,
We wandered to an upland slope
  And knelt among the lichen?

The sunlight through the trees
  Showed touch of Autumn splendor,
The marsh flowers glowed like fire among
  The grasses fresh and tender.

I'll keep that day's fair splendor,
  Which all my soul did win,
With Autumn Blooms, and Dear Brown Eyes
  That let the sunshine in.

September 9th.

TO ——

You need not question if the past
  Sweeps o'er my soul to-day;
The memory of that morn must last
  Through cloud and shine, alway.

No morn can ever fairer be,
  Nor day, howe'er complete,
Than when my soul awoke and found
  My treasure true and sweet.

October 5, 1887-89.

"SO KEEP MY MEMORY GREEN."

TO ——

"So keep my memory green,"
  Is all you'd ask of me?
I could not have a fonder charge
  For all the years to be,

For all the unknown future
  In the distant hidden years,
To keep my heart from sorrowing,
  To charm away my tears,

Than the boon that memory gives
  Through the love-light of its lays,
Than just the joy of looking back
  To count the golden days;

To mark where first thy sunlight
  Made rift within the cloud,
And bade my darkened soul look up
  And be no longer bowed;

To count the tiny chords
  Love touched and woke to song,
To know just how the music came,
  From notes that slept so long.

'Twill float a-down life's morning,
  And brighten all life's day, '
'Twill gild the evening shadows
  As the daylight fades away;

And when in darkened silence
  Life's loves shall all depart,
And life itself shall ebb away
  From out my tired heart,

As the shadows fall and thicken,
  And I touch the twilight gray,
When my fluttering soul breaks forth at last
  From out its home of clay,

I'll clasp and keep forever
  Thy memory's golden sheen,
And in the far, far future
  Thou shalt find it fair and green.

PICTURES.

TO ———

In the warmth and glow of evening fire-light
  I am sitting, dear, with thoughts of you
Pressing closely through the fading twilight,
  Falling softly as the silent dew.

Making pictures such as painters dream of,
  Pictures such as artist never drew,
Touched with color, life and light, that seem of
  Something far beyond the painter knew.

Woods and fields, and all the pleasant places,
  Dearest haunts my feet have trod with you,
Meadow-lands aglow with flowering graces,
  Wildering hedges where the sweetest blew.

Come with summer sunset's golden glances,
  Happy talks by brook and garden wall,
Crowned with treasures from the poet's fancies,
  Love, that shed a halo over all.

These are pictures that the gloaming brings me,
 While the evening shadows come and go;
With a song the silence softly sings me
 Music from the unseen, soft and low.

So, dear, through the frosty Winter twilight
 Love keeps fresh the last year's buds and flowers,
And brings again, across the Winter firelight,
 The splendor of the golden Summer hours.

MELODY.

My soul was wakened when first you spoke
 In a voice so sweet and low;
It heard and knew as the morning broke
 In the flush of love's first glow.

Over my heart your tenderness swept,
 Like a breath from a sunny clime,
Drying the tears my soul had wept
 With the music of love's low rhyme.

A music that drifted across the waste
 Of days with never a song,
Till the echoes of love my heart embraced
 Made melody all the day long.

A MESSAGE.

I send to you, dear, this balmy morn,
  A message whose burden your heart will know,
A song without words o'er the silence sent,
  Low notes, to be borne on the west wind's flow.

You will know that it comes direct from me,
  As it kisses your cheek and forehead fair,
And lingers to touch in its flight your lips
  Ere its last caress in your warm brown hair.

HEART ECHOES.

I have wished thee well, in the dear, dead past,
  And the future can hold no fairer flowers
Within the clasp of its sweetest years
  Than the past has hid in its buried bowers.

No warmer love can gild the hours
  That may follow the wake of the days that are dead
Than the tender gleam from the shadowy past
  Of all I've thought, or dreamed, or said.

I can only add to the dreams for you
    The fairest gift that can come from me,
A love that may brighten the future hours,
    And light all the days of the years to be.

January 21st.

WHEN THE SUMMER DIES.

I shall miss you, love, in the coming days,
        When the summer is dead;
I shall want your help in the lonely ways
        My feet must tread.

I shall hunger oft for a kindly look,
        Or a word low spoken,
And shall long again for the days that partook
        Of love's sweet token.

My heart through the silence will call you, dear,
        In the days that must fall,
And I know that your own will feel me a-near
        And hear the call.

I shall know if you answer, though none may hear
        The whisper that floats
From the far off song that must dry my tears
        With its faithful notes.

I shall know, be it morn or eventide
    When the echoes wake,
For my heart in its beating will stop to hide
    The love it will take.

MILE-STONES.

Another birthday greets thee, love,
    Wherein to wish thee well;
Another dawn upon the marge
    Of Time's broad circling swell,

Across whose margin could I write
    All that its hours could hold,
The fay's rich gifts could scarcely vie
    With the joys it should enfold.

Within the present, now thine own,
    No shadow should abide;
The future should all cloudless be,
    And fair life's eventide.

January 21, 1880.

REVERIES.

There's a gloom that hovers o'er me
    While I sit and muse alone ;
There's a sadness lingers near me
    Wherever I may roam,

In the busy haunts of pleasure,
    Through the solitude of night,
In the coming hours of leisure,
    In the misty soft twilight,

Still pursues this blighting sorrow
    That crushed my joyous heart
In the days when each to-morrow
    Seemed for me a happy part.

.   .   .   .

Ah! musings of my mother,
    Of an angel form that fled!
Ah! dreams that clasp and cover
    The faces of our dead!

Beyond you in the waking,
    Away from sorrow's night,
When freed from earthly aching,
    Our hearts shall find the light.

HEART-ACHE.

I could not speak with your face so near,
  Though I knew the summer days would sleep;
My words would form, and falter and fall
  Unspoken, because my heart would weep.

Do you think, in the days that drifted by,
  With only the music your singing wrought,
That I loved you less, though the songs were few,
  When love was the song your singing brought?

Your precious gifts I keep in sight:
  Their treasured sweetness mutely tells
Of a love that was mine, mine only, dear,
  Till I missed the music of fairy bells.

Life's path is short, love's way is long;
  'Twill reach beyond the summer days
When our lips are still, and our hands are clasped,
  And our tired feet have learned other ways.

MAY BLOSSOMS.

These buds and blossoms that I send you, dear,
  The fragrance of the summer hours enfold;
May all that's brightest, best within the year
  Lie hidden underneath the sweets they hold.

Born of the sunshine and the soft south wind,
  I send them with a greeting warm and true;
May every blossom bear a tender thought
  In all the balmy sweets they take to you.

WHEN DO YOU THINK OF ME MOST?

When do you think of me most, dear,
  Through all the hours of day?
Is it when the morning's rosy light
  Is chasing the shadows away?

Do I come to you then, or do I wait
  Till the noontide's drowsy hour,
Climbing the stairs of your fancy, love,
  In your day-dream's castle tower?

Perchance when the day is dying, dear,
  Your spirit encircles mine,
And welcomes me most in the gloaming, sweet,
  When the day and night combine.

TO THE PICTURE OF LONGFELLOW'S CHILDREN.

Grouped in a trio before me
  Three faces sweet and fair:
"Grave Alice and laughing Allegra,
  And Edith, with golden hair,"

Look out from the halo of childhood
  Into these eyes of mine—
Three gems of rarest promise
  Decking a poet's shrine.

Three faces aglow with sunshine
  From the cloudless sky of youth,
Telling the first sweet story
  From the years of love and truth.

Three jewels of priceless value
  For a poet's heart to wear:
" Grave Alice and laughing Allegra,
  And Edith, with golden hair."

INTUITION.

I looked on the moon at its full,
  The moon that looked down on me,
In response to the many sweet fancies
  My heart was sending to thee.

And I wondered, as upward they circled,
  If thy soul had power to see,
And could read from the face of fair Luna
  The fancies there written by me.

If it did, and the moon told truly.
  "What answer did'st thou send me?"
Ah! deary, the moonbeams told it,
  The message: "I'm thinking of thee."

November 16, 1880.

SING OF THE FLOWERS.

The sunshine is kissing with warm, glad light
Our eyelids to waking from winter's long night:
The dewdrops are waiting a chrism to place
In jewels of splendor on garments of grace.

The south wind is calling, we know he's a-near ;
We wait his caresses to welcome us here ;
Fair blossoms we'll scatter of purple and gold,
And the earth shall rejoice with the incense we hold.

Earth's stars we are called, shining under the skies,
Lighting meadow and mountain with rainbow dyes,
Shedding brightness and beauty with lessons of peace
That shall cling to the earth when our blossoms shall cease.

Then welcome us back from our slumber and dreams ;
We are born of the sunshine, we bring you its beams ;
In daffodil splendor, and violet bloom,
We brighten the earth and banish its gloom.

PILGRIMAGE.

When first our feet are placed on Life's broad pathway,
  Fair flowers, molded by a master-hand,
Scattered broadcast where e'er our footsteps wander,
  Illume the pathway to the silent land.

As on we further tread, the heart grows 'wildered,
  Seeking an outlet from a labyrinth wild ;
The flowers that bloomed so tenderly at dawning,
  At eve with thorns will wound the weary child.

The warm, quick throb that in our pulses lingers
  Tells but the story of the heart's unrest,
Speaks but the yearning of the tired pilgrim
  To reach the shining " Islands of the blest. "

And as we wait, the mists of eve grow fainter,
  While through the haze there floats a golden light,
Pointing the spirit with an unseen finger
  Out of the shadow unto the shining height.

UNATTAINED.

We are always living in hope,
  We are ever looking afar,
We are always peering through darkness
  For the light of our favorite star.

Sometimes we catch glimmers of brightness
  Through rifts in the clouds of our night,
And it seems that the morning is breaking
  With gladness, and beauty, and light.

And so, to some hearts it comes laden,
  But to others, so burdened with tears,
That the light of their lives seems hidden
  In the cloud of their sorrowing years.

But 'tis ever to hope through our weeping,
  Though the darkness of night covers all,
And the morn of our lives still finds us
  Buried deep in the folds of its pall.

INCOMPLETENESS.

Out of our lives we miss some note,
  Something of melody fails us here;
Over the heart-strings floats a mist,
  Out of the music falls a tear.

Something of melody out of the song,
  From the tremulous notes of the old refrain
Something of weariness drifted in,
  Something very akin to pain

Comes with the scent of the dewy cowslips,
  Blown from the meadows all a-bloom,
Lives in the breath of the sweet red clover
  Drifted in silence across the gloom.

Over the music, and buds, and blossoms,
  A shadow falls that closely clings,
A something very akin to sorrow,
  A discord that trembles amid the strings.

SONNET.

When, from your earth-dream to that other life,
  Touched by some soft-palmed seraph, you shall wake,
  When Heaven's fair splendor on your soul shall break,
Far from the babble of earth's jarring strife,
In that new clime, with radiant glory rife,
  Will you, amid such joy, once long to take
  My heart within your clasp, to soothe the ache,
Left captive in its clay, and moaning for your sake?
It may be you will miss some low, sweet word,
  And stoop to reach the love that once was yours,
Before your soul had listened for and heard
  That sweeter music floating down that lures
The spirit from its clay, whose fetters gird
  Only for a space the soul that clay endures.

LINES TO G. H. C.

The sweet summer-time, with its fair June roses
  And sweet-scented blossoms, lies dead at our feet,
But robed like a queen, with pale hands folded,
  In purple and gold for a winding-sheet.

The overblown roses, that fell from her clasping
  Lie on her heart with a meaning untold—
All that is left for the heart that is silent,
  An incense that falls over purple and gold.

Let not the roses of life droop and wither,
  With all of their tenderness left unsaid,
Ere the summer-time dies, with its passionate longing,
  And the heart cease to hope when the summer is dead.

MY BOAT.

I built myself a magic boat
  That drifted out to sea,
Bearing away on the wavelets' float
  All that was dear to me.

It danced and rocked on the ocean wave
  As the winds blew light and free;
The white sails sped to some ocean cave,
  And my boat was hid from me.

It will never, Oh! never, come back to me,
  And the waves a secret keep;
Far down its treasure lies hid in the sea,
  'Neath the ocean mosses deep.

And the sea-weed green waves over it all,
　While the salt-sands heave and moan
For the treasure sunk fathoms beyond recall—
　For the bark that was all my own.

WE TWO.

Once in a summer not long gone,
　We two made dreams for golden weather,
We two clasped hands and sat us down
　Beside the summer days together.

The air a thousand perfumes bore
　From meadow-lands afar and near,
The woods a thousand anthems sung,
　So well they knew the summer near,

The sweet June days, when roses bloom
　And daisies show their golden hearts,
When nature seems a-tune with man,
　And man in tune with nature's arts.

But clouds lay hid within the days,
　And storms behind the sunny weather,
Our hands unclasped, might came between,
　And severed hearts so bound together.

MRS. BROWNING.

And she, the magic minstrel, still sings on;
  The echo of her melody flows in
  On every wind that sighs, and o'er the din
Of earth the low mysterious music rings on
Hearts athirst for love, her mystic Eon.
  The tuneful hand that swept love's lyre lies deep in
  Dust; yet earth is filled with strains Æolian,
Still trembling with the fire of life's vibration,
  Struck from the harp that only knew her touch.
    A-down the infinite float new anthems, ringing
      Clearly above the tones of moan and mirth;
Earth's choristers are mute while hearing such,
  And seraphs, 'neath their palm-trees sweetly singing,
    Hear naught more sweet than notes she left to earth.

VIOLETS.

TO MADGE.

Faded, and yet so fragrant,
  Crushed, and faded, and dead,
Yet fragrant of happy memories
  In the faintest breath they shed.

Pressed and kept for the love's sake
   Hid in their tiny leaves,
Forming the thread so golden
   In the loom where memory weaves.

Laden with the melody
   Of voices that are no more,
Fraught with the music sweeping
   The heart-strings o'er and o'er.

Sad music as it rises
   In sobs from the faded flowers,
Sad music in its wailing
   For the hearts no longer ours.

Oh! pale and fragrant flowerets,
   Ye waken from their sleep
Bright dreams, with shadows mingled
   From out the misty deep.

HOW?

How shall I fashion a song from the summer,
  Waken sweet notes from days that are dead,
Bring back the scent of the sweet June roses,
  Call back the music of sweet words said?

How shall I call again out from the shadows
  Long sunny days, when the sunsets grew red,
Hours when the shadows grew long on the hillsides,
  Hiding the valleys when daylight had fled?

Tread through the corridors love has so hallowed,
  Waken the harp upon memory's walls,
Note upon note from chamber to chamber
  Echo sweet music through memory's halls.

List! How it sings of the blossoming June-time,
  The summer that lingered but could not stay,
Lovingly lingered in sweet orchard closes,
  Left in the woodlands a blessing for aye.

Thus do I fashion a song from the summer,
  A soulful song from the summer that died,
From the melody left in the heart of the valleys,
  And dreams that flow in with the eventide.

HER PORTRAIT.

Darling May,
Light of day,
Chasing shadows far away!

With surprise
From brownest eyes
Where a love-light ever lies!

Holding looks,
Like meadow brooks,
Where the sunshine finds the nooks!

In her face
A tender grace
Leads one captive, to a place

Near her heart,
To share a part
Never found in other mart.

How to tell
The magic spell
She wields, in winning hearts so well,

Ask the flowers
In the bowers
Why the sunshine and the showers

Ope their eyes
To sunny skies—
There the secret sweetly lies!

True and sweet
The looks you'll meet,
If she turn your face to greet.

Faith renewing,
Ever doing
All the lips could tell in wooing.

True and tried,
She's sweetest guide;
Her love will crown life's eventide.

One could never
Wish to sever
From her heart for aye and ever.

May love enfold her
In all I've told her,
And love and I forever hold her!

POND LILIES.

Oh, lilies, fair starlings, ye hold me in thrall!
  Your magic uncurtains the past;
Ye bear me memories sweeter than dreams,
  Such dreams as may not last.

Ah! fairy touch of a wand unseen
  From petals now faded and dead!
Mute singers, ye waken a melody new
  In a heart whence the music had fled

Of first fair days when love awoke
  In the heart with a new-born joy
A memory of reeds by a river's brink—
  A boat,—a girl,—a boy,—

Green lily-pads with their freighted bloom
  That dimpled the waters, cool,
And the mossy banks where we told our love
  Beside the silvery pool.

Oh, fair pond lilies! Who fashioned the spell
  That binds with a music low?
Would ye could hold me fettered for aye
  With my love of a long ago!

TO ——

Deal no unkind or cruel blow
  To wound the human heart.
For years may come and years may go,
  It still retains the smart.

Though time may heal, it leaves a scar
  Which yields to every breath;
It trembles with the slightest jar,
  And vibrates unto death.

It gives sad music to the world
  When once its strings are broken,
It yields a wail when its chords are swept
  By a word unkindly spoken.

It echoes the breath in anger hurled,
  And breathes to the night its cries,
And e'en in dreams its secret grieving
  Betrays itself in sighs.

A CHRISTMAS GREETING.

In the pearly hours of dawning,
  Between the gray and blue,
    A thought was born
    For Christmas morn,
  And the thought, dear, was of you.

I thought of the gifts that others
  Would fashion with dainty grace,

With greetings born
For Christmas morn
That time could ne'er efface.

And I thought of the gift I'd send you,
'Twas one I'd sent before,
When Christmas morn
Was sweetly born,
A Christmas-tide of yore.

But take the gift I send you,
Though not a work of art,
For Christmas morn
Just newly born—
I simply send my heart.

HER ROOM.

A sound like notes at dawning,
From song of distant birds,
Comes floating down the silence,
A song of two sweet words:

Two words—to wake from dreaming,
Of palms and distant seas,
Of blooms of purple heather
And scent of flowery leas:

Two words—to break my slumbers
  From dreamy night to day,
A magic song to charm me,
  To make November May:

"Her Room!" What haven like it?
  A refuge of delight;
No clouds abide within it,
  Her sunshine makes it bright.

INDIAN SUMMER.

A haze on the land, and a dream on the heart,
  A silence of mist on the hillside brown,
A rosy light through the twinkling mist,
  A drowsy air o'er a sleepy town;

A rosy mist enwrapping the days,
  "The calm, mild days" that autumn holds,
Bringing the summer again to our hearts,
  And hiding it there in its rosy folds;

A "Lotus Land" where we sit us down
  On the golden sands to eat and dream;
We sit us down where the tired fields,
  And the weary woods, and the singing stream

Have rest from toil as we who sing
　Thro' the "Summer of Saints" that crowns the year
With its sunny hours and amber skies,
　And all that a summer holds so dear.

A "Lotus Land," and the dreamers we,
　Resting from toil on the golden sands,
Bringing us nearer the magic gate
　That leads our hearts to the sunset lands.

SEEDLINGS.

Among the relics of by-gone days
　Lay seedlings garnered by tired hands;
A summer slept in the wee brown bits,
　Waiting to tell of sunny lands.

A blushing bloom lay hid in the dark,
　A prescient fragrance of flowery May
Slept through the hours of a starless night,
　Awaiting the sunshine and glory of day.

Fair visions were dreamed of a blossoming grace,
　While they held the secret still unsung
Of ferns, and mosses, and woodland streams,
　Of mountain heights when the year was young;

Till the sunlight touched with its magic wand
  The sleeping bits with a tender ray,
And kissed to life from the winter of sleep
  The spring-time and fragrance of flowery May.

———————

BIRTHDAY FLOWERS.

A message within the folded leaves,
  A secret hid in the petals fair,
A signet pressed 'neath purple wings,
  A seal my soul must ever wear;

A dear remembrance fitly hidden
  My heart will find in the blossoms gay,
A fragrance of thought in the sweetness sleeping,
  An incense of love to cherish for aye.

March 6th.

———————

TO MRS. ——

All through the hours of this quaint morn
A fairy song comes faintly borne,
Telling my heart, in love's own way,
Of a Some One who strayed into life one day;

Some one whose coming made glad the earth,
While old Saint Valentine sung at her birth;
Some one to scatter the sunshine and flowers,
Some one to brighten the darkest hours,

Waked to the light one gladsome day,
And hid in her heart the blossoms of May,
Keeping them fresh for the years to be,
And drifting their sweets in a song to me.

February 14th.

SAINT VALENTINE.

This curious date of Cupid's chart
Was graven once on a maiden's heart,
  In the days when love was young,
And ever since, as the year rolls round,
With maidens all this date is found
  With the song that love first sung.

"From me to thee, O faithful heart,
Forever thine till death us part,
  Forever, ever thine!"
Through all the world this self-same day
Is ringing still; this self-same lay
  Still sings Saint Valentine.

A DREAM RECALLED.

As 'tween the silent hours of day and dawn
  My spirit lay within the hush of sleep,
In that pale twilight ere the night had gone,
  And day trod down the darkness with her feet.

As one by one the golden stars grew pale
  Within the ether's dim expanse of blue,
Ere dawn had broke the night's mysterious vail,
  Into my soul a dream came shining through.

Within the borders of that pale shadow-land
  My spirit viewed you, sitting midst a throng
Of white-winged seraphs, and with lifted hand
  Beckoning me near to hear the seraph's song.

Sweet music floated like a distant murmur,
  And the song I heard was chanted soft and low:
"We are the guardian angels whose love enfolds her,
  To shield and comfort her while here below."

Vainly I tried to enter at the portal,
  In vain my empty arms reached out to you;
There seemed no room for any form of mortal
  Save yours, whereon I looked, while softer grew

Those notes of love and tenderness that drew me
  Closer, but, ah, too far to touch your hand!
Yet waiting, all expectant, for a voice to lead me
  Close to your side amid that guardian band.

Amid the silence, from my weary heart
  Aloud I told my sorrow to the night:
"She has so many, alone I must depart!"
  When, lo! from out the dream your love brought light.

———————

TO C. C. H. AT SEA.

Break now the seal of greeting,
  Sweet friend upon the sea;
Unfold from out the darkness
  The thoughts I send to thee.

Though last, I pray you count me
  Not least among the throng,
Whose notes across the silence
  Now wake to friendship's song.

Life's fairest benedictions
  I sing thee evermore,
"*Bon voyage*" on the waters
  That stretch from shore to shore.

The sea that now divides us
   Keeps only hands apart,
No boundless sweep of ocean
   Can sever heart from heart.

Nor times nor seasons alter
   The love of friend for friend,
The bond that brightens ever,
   Abiding to the end.

——————

SOMEBODY LOVES ME IN DREAMS.

Yes, somebody loves me in dreams,
   And I fancy your heart could tell
Who it is that calls me "Darling,"
   Who it is that loves me so well.

But the name I never will mention,
   For I've strictly promised to keep
This pretty secret of dreamland
   Where no one but I may peep.

For the welcome of loving smiles
   And words that are tender and true,
With sometimes the clasp of a soft, warm palm,
   And a kiss to banish life's rue.

How strange and sweet to be loved!
　　To be loved as in fancy it seems,
To know that you're somebody's darling,
　　Though somebody loves but in dreams;

To feel that life is all sunshine,
　　With nothing to banish its beams,
To drink at the sweetest of fountains,
　　Though only drinking in dreams.

"THREE-SCORE AND TEN."

It seems but yester e'en
　　Since youth and I kissed lips
Across life's sunny stream.

Lightly we kissed, nor wept
　　At parting so forever,
As on the river swept.

In vain I call: "Come back,
　　My sunny, sunny youth,
Across life's frozen track!"

The weary years have flown
　　That drifted us apart,
And I am left alone.

With three-score years and ten,
  And youth forever fled,
My days go sadly on.

Waiting the twilight's beam,
  "I lay me down to sleep,"
And cross life's troubled stream.

FOREVER.

Forever, and forever!
  Long covenant to make,
    For hearts of clay,
    To bravely say:
  "Naught can our faith e'er break
Forever, and forever."

Yet hearts that love sing thus
  Love's lullaby complete;
    We say and sing,
    And offerings bring
  Close to our idol's feet,
Whose love so clings to us.

Forever, and forever!
  When the years are laid to sleep,

As the ages go,
I will love you so,
Love's covenant to keep
Forever, and forever!

———

IN VAIN.

We look in vain for the roses
  That bloomed in the hedges low,
In vain through the scentless meadows,
  The west winds softly blow.

They can not waken the flowers
  From their deep and silent sleep,
Where they fell in their quiet beauty
  In the glen and on the steep.

With their fragrance departed the summer,
  And their bloom that gladdened the hills;
The west wind sighs in his searching
  For the flowers that fringed the rills.

The vines and the faded blossoms,
  That lie so mute at our feet,
Are only the sad reminders
  Of flowers that once were sweet.

DE PROFUNDIS.

Only the wail of an erring human heart
  Borne by the ether wave to touch thine ear;
Why close the portals of thine inner self?
  Why stoop not low thy kindred's grief to hear,

Calling from out the deep, "For mercy's sake,
  Bear with me yet a little longer here;
Crush not to earth the bruised and broken vine,
  Trailing so low in anguish and in fear?"

Call from its source the word of pity blest;
  Ope the warm fountain of tender human tears;
Hearts that are aching needs must slowly break;
  Ah! pluck the thorns from out the weary years.

Give from thy store of love some word of peace;
  Thy gift shall prove a blessing unto thee
In hours of darkness, when the shadows fall,
  A light for all the years that are to be.

SONG WORDS.

DRIFTING.

TO A. E. B.

Drifting slowly, slowly drifting
  Through the shadowy realm of years,
Some are drifting through the sunlight,
  Others through a mist of tears,
    Bitter, blinding tears.

Drifting through the filmy vapors,
  Reaching for the sunny rays,
Dreaming as they're slowly wafted,
  Dreaming of the happy days,
    Lost and happy days.

Oh! how sadly, vainly calling
  For the days that are no more!
Aching hearts are holding only
  Echoes from the fading shore,
    Echoes, nothing more!

ANSWERED.

Oh, Jamie, the breezes are blowing
  My wishes far over the sea!
Do you hear them, my Jamie? They're saying,
  "Come back to your own by the Dee!"
The hills miss your music and murmur,
  From their purple there floats down to me
The song that the valley is singing
  To the river that flows to the sea.

The brightness has gone from the morning,
  And the days overshadowed will be,
Till we meet where we parted, my Jamie,
  On the banks of the sweet River Dee.
Oh, Jamie, alone I am weeping,
  Your answer has flown back to me;
"We shall meet as we parted, my darling,
  But not on the banks of the Dee!"

LULLABY—REST.

Hushaby, hushaby, softly we sing,
Hushaby, eventide, slumber will bring;
  Bird in the downy nest,

Babe on the mother's breast,
Sweetly earth's weary rest
Under night's wing.

Hushaby, heart of mine, slumber will come;
Patience, the eventide comes to us all;
Sunset and lullaby,
Clasped hands and hushaby,
Silent the heart cry,
Sweet—rest for all.

BIRD AND WIND.

Oh, wind of the South,
Blow gently this way,
Gently, this way!

Oh, nightingale, sing what my lover would say,
Sing it, I pray;
And trust to the south wind to wait it this way,
Wait me the words of his mouth!
My heart waits the message; oh, make no delay,
Bird and wind of the South!

DONALD.

Oh, list to me, dear!
From afar you are near;
You come to my dreams on the wings of sleep;
    You follow the wake
    That my day-dreams make
Over the span of the mystic deep.

    You sit at my side,
    And naught can betide,
Though a ghostly hand I clasp ere-while,
    For I feed on the dew
    Of a love so true,
No shadow can darken the light of your smile.

WHEN THE YEAR GROWS OLD.

He left me when the summer,
  Grown tired of her reign,
Laid down her royal scepter
  Amid the golden grain;
When the reapers with their sickles
  Garnered up the autumn's gold.
He left a troth-kiss on my lips,
  And softly sang the story old.

"And fare you well, my own,
  A short farewell," sang he;
"Again the year grows old,
  I'll be, my love, with thee."
But thrice the autumn's gold has burned,
  And thrice the year has tired grown,
And yet my love comes not to me,
  For lips are still that sang "my own."

SAILING.

There's a bark on the deep;
    It is sailing away,
    Sailing away,
And the moon's looking down with a silvery ray,
    A silvery ray,
On one who is sailing far out on the bay,
    While mother and I must weep.
Oh! shine on his track with the light of day,
    For father sails over the deep.

MY KING.

I had thought, with the roses of June,
  That my love would come back to me;
I had dreamed of two hearts atune,
  Floating out on a summer sea,
  That mystical summer sea.

At gloaming I watched for the sail
  That should bear my love to the shore,
But the sunset's gold grew pale,
  And the sea moaned "nevermore,"
  And the cliffs sighed "nevermore!"

Yet my heart from its silent tower
  Is still looking over the sea,
For my King, with his magical power,
  Who will some time come back to me,
  Bringing love and life to me.

OCEAN LETTERS.

TO K. D.

Dear Kate:—I know your fancy
  For letters extra brief,
And trust my humble efforts
  Upon this tiny leaf
May prove an innovation,
  Supplying all your need
Of love and loyal friendship
  From a small American Weed;
And among the English flowers
  Your heart will soon embrace,
Let none efface the memory,
  And none usurp the place
You've given the humble blossom
  You leave this side of the sea,
Nor break the bond of friendship
  Your love has forged for me.
From out the vanished hours,
  Now hidden in the past,
An incense will awaken
  From memories that must last

As long as life shall give me
  New days, and months, and years,
With time for joy and gladness,
  And the sadder time for tears—
A fragrance that will heighten
  The joys, while joys abide,
And lessen all life's shadows,
  Till falls life's eventide.
Songs that the heart may fashion
  Reflect the music there;
The sweetness yours has sung me
  But makes my own more fair.
And now, what time in silence
  Your heart may sit alone,
Counting upon the ocean
  The friends you call your own,
Turn back, my ocean rover,
  Turn heart-warm to the West,
And whisper through the stillness
  The names you love the best.
Do not forget the "Circle"
  Your presence made complete
In a fair New England village,
  Where hearts shall hope to greet
The friend whose absence darkens,
  Whose coming will relight
The days that must be shadowed
  Till Love's returning flight.

And now, dear Kate, a message
  To yours beyond the sea,
A message of remembrance
Direct from mine and me,
  And to yourself, in closing,
Find " Farewell " and " God-speed,"
  With love enough to bring you back
To your warm friends,

SISTERS WEED.

Greenwich, Conn. ·

TO C. C. H.

Dear " Neal" :— When your hand shall essay to unfold
The thoughts which my love herein has enrolled,
As you rock on the deep, may your spirit be stirred
With echoes from home hid away in each word.
Look back through the hours of the long summer days,
And may fancy paint pictures to gladden your gaze
Of kindred and friends whose love and devotion
Have borne you companionship over the ocean
And will follow you all through the hours of each day
With wishes, heart-warm, that will shine on your way,
Be it over the pave of a gay city street,
Or afar from the sound of hurrying feet,
Along the Rhine Valley or Switzer's fair hills,
By green English meadows or Erin's clear rills,

Or into the heart of Italia's dear bowers,
Where the nightingale sings through the moonlight and
        flowers,
Or wherever your wandering footsteps may lead,
With our love, dear, we'll faithfully wish you "God-speed."
But amid all the beauty of change and surprise,
Which may greet you while dwelling 'neath far alien skies,
Send back to the land and the friends left behind
A memory of scenes your heart had enshrined,
Ere you bade us adieu in the "Home of the free,"
To wander awhile in the " Land o'er the sea."
Forget not, dear Neal, the hours of good cheer
We spent in a cottage while you were anear,
Our long, pleasant chats when the eventide fell,
Our jolly late talks, till the midnight bell
Warned us both to our slumber for sake of our health,
Or, as sages have written, to get to us wealth ;
But, whatever the reason, we finished the night
In slumbers so peaceful we wakened as bright
As if all the hours the night calls her own
Had been hidden in dreams till the shadows had flown.
Then remember the drive to "Belle Haven beach,"
On that morning of beauty beyond human speech,
When nature, designing to win us, complete
In her loveliest garments knelt at our feet,
Beguiling our hearts and winning us quite,
As we sat on the beach in the sand so white,
With the tide coming in 'neath the blue summer sky,

On that fair morn in June-time, dear Neal, you and I.
And again, when at "Hawthorne," what joy was our own,
As we gathered the shells while we talked quite alone,
Looking out on the bay which, in jest, we dubbed Naples,
Where the waves kissed the shore lined with beeches and
      maples.
Do you think, dear, whatever new beauty may meet you,
You will find dearer scenes than at home used to greet you?
Some fairer you'll find, perhaps, but none dearer,
Though the skies may be brighter, the streams may be clearer.
There is naught in the world, wherever you roam,
That can equal the beauty and dearness of home.
You may walk by the Seine, and visit the Rhone,
You may view the rich beauty of Bois de Boulogne,
Ere you seek pastures new on the far Alpine hills,
Whose glory with rapture the heart ever fills,
Or your steps lead you southward to Venice or Rome,
Ere your hearts and your faces again turn to home,
But turn your heart back ere you reach the far shore,
For while reading these lines, will your journey be o'er.
Send over the waters that fill the deep sea
Some sign that "My Neal" is thinking of me.
And now, with "Adieu," best wishes be yours,
On this or on any of life's varied tours,
With health and good speed till the journey shall last,
And a harbor of safety to rest in at last;
Good bye, and pray let not this billet condemn me,
But believe me, with love, dearest Neal,

                    Your own "EMMIE."

Greenwich, Conn.

CHRISTMAS LETTER.

TO MISS N.

I have not forgotten my promise, Miss N.,
To furnish you something direct from my pen,
And though late in the season some chronicles show
That the warmest thoughts oft come with the snow.
At least let me hope that my honest intention
May embody a sentiment worthy of mention,
And that you, in recalling some thoughts of the past
Reflected in this, may find one that shall last
Beyond all the chances and changes of time.
Be it summer or winter, you honor my rhyme
With a glance at its meaning quite worthy the theme,
Of a friendship engendering the warmest esteem.
Enough, if these lines shall prove how sincere
Is the memory I've kept and shall ever hold dear.
I have thought of the days in the summer gone by,
And wondered if ever again you and I
Would meet and renew, in the same pleasant places,
The same pleasant talks, and see the same faces,
With the circle unbroken by sorrow or change,
And if friends we knew then could ever grow strange.
Such fancies will come as the seasons go round,
And we find ourselves dreaming of friends we have found;
New links in the chain that bind hearts together,

That tarnish nor rust not in life's stormy weather.
The Christmas-tide glory falls low as I write,
But my heart in its wishing looks up through a light,
And sends o'er the distance that keeps us apart
The wish that life's blessings may gladden your heart.
Let me hope for you ever no sorrow may trouble you,
And you find a new link in the love of

E. W.

Greenwich, Conn.

THE SLEEPING BEAUTY.

Many and many long years ago,
Where the forest flowers were wont to blow
    Within an ancient wood,
Long hidden from the waking world,
With trumpet stilled and banner furled,
    A grand old castle stood.

No sound within the castle walls,
No note was echoed through the halls,
    No sign of life was heard,
While all without was cold and still
As water of a frozen rill.
    Nor grass nor leaflet stirred.

A charm of fairy night and power
That covered castle, wall and tower,
    At midnight on it fell,

Which doomed a hundred years of sleep
To seal in slumber, long and deep,
　　The court by fairy spell.

The cause of such enchantment rare
Was wrought through Princess, young and fair,
　　Within the castle old,
Who, dreaming late one winter night
Beside the ember's fitful light,
　　Espied a key of gold,

Which quickly from the fire she drew,
And on her ermine robe she threw,
　　To try the magic power.
Through distant halls of oaken floor,
By many a winding corridor,
　　She sped at midnight hour.

And while the king and nobles all
Within the castle's festive hall
　　The banquet hour were keeping,
The Princess, on her lonely quest,
Forgetting king and noble guest,
　　Beguiled the hours of sleeping.

And on through many a secret way,
Deep hidden from the light of day,
　　The magic key she bore,

Till, glancing through a gallery wide
That led to turret, she espied
    An ancient studded door.

Within the lock of curious mold
The Princess placed the key of gold,
    Seeking the tower to win.
With trembling hand the bolt she sprung,
And loudly through the castle rung
    The sound of midnight din.

Buried beneath the dust of years
The narrow stairway there appears,
    Leading to turret high,
Where, in the moonlit chamber lone,
Spinning, there sat a withered crone,
    Ne'er seen by mortal eye,

Till on that lonely winter night,
Beneath the moonbeams dusty light,
    The Princess first descried her
Engaged with distaff, fleece and reel,
And spindle formed of burnished steel,
    That drew the maid beside her.

Who, gazing, longed to twine the thread
Around the spindle's shining head
    And guide the skein so slender.

When, lo! the hand in haste to spin
Just touched the polished pointed pin,
   Which pierced the palm so tender.

Within, without, a silence deep,
Borne on the shadowy wings of sleep,
   Wrapt all in close embrace—
The king and guest in banquet hall,
The restless steed within his stall,
   The warder at his place.

And on an ivory couch was laid,
In sleep, the Princess, peerless maid,
   Beneath a silken cover,
Where, softened to a sweet repose,
The snowy bosom sunk and rose
   In dreams of coming lover.

The pale, sweet cuckoo flowers blew,
The crocus bloomed, the daisies grew,
   The primrose blushed and died,
And still within that castle old,
Within that grim and ancient hold,
   No signs of life abide.

A hundred times the fragrant spring
Silently folded its perfumed wing.
   A hundred summers waned,

A hundred autumns poured their gold
Into earth's coffers manifold,
    A hundred winters reigned.

The charm had spent its fatal power,
A Prince had dreamed of castle bower
    Wherein the Princess lay,
And, mounted on a gallant steed,
With vow to "answer Lady's need,"
    The Prince pursued his way.

Resolved to ride without repose
Till on his sight the castle rose
    Like vision of his dream,
He journeyed on by day and night,
By rosy dawn and fading light,
    Through vale, and mount, and stream.

At last, as in a mist, he sees
Above the green of forest trees
    The castle's ancient towers,
And, pressing on through grasses dank,
He spurs his courser's foaming flank,
    Through marsh and wildwood flowers.

The golden beams of fading day
Gilded the battlement grim and gray,
    And kissed the princely crest,

As through the arched and massive gate
The Prince rode on to find, though late,
   The object of his quest.

With beating heart 'neath shield of gold
Royally rode that knight of old
   Into the courtyard lone,
Where, echoing through the silent place,
The sound of hoof-falls' measured pace
   Fell on the courtyard stone.

He leaves the court, he gains the stairs,
He seeks the "Bower of Lady fair;"
   Through many a wildering way
Love leads; he follows far and fast.
The chamber door is reached at last,
   Love crowns the fading day.

Into the dimly lighted room,
Where perfumed tapers broke the gloom,
   Entered the princely lover.
The slumbrous air was softly stirred,
Yet naught the sleeping Princess heard
   Beneath the broidered cover.

The gallant Knight stooped low to take
One lingering look 'ere he should break
   The charm within his keeping.

Then nearer to the peerless face
He leaned, the pledge of love to place
  On lips so fair in sleeping.

The charm was spent, the spell was broke,
That fervent kiss the Princess woke,
  Love's touch aroused the sleeper;
Love's summons rang through bower and hall,
Love's echoes waked the slumberers all,
  From king to lowly keeper.

All waked as years before all slept;
A moment broke what years had kept,
  And loosed the bonds forever;
A dream, a kiss, had wrought so much,
All yielded to love's magic touch,
  And crowned love's brave endeavor.

CAPTURE OF STONY POINT BY GEN. WAYNE,

JULY 16, 1779.

The tramp of heroes since high noon
Was heard on mountain steep and through ravine,
And the dull echoes frighted from their lairs
The timid races of the wood and brake.

Onward they trod, nor wearied in the march
Through deep morass and over pathless height
That lay 'twixt them and victory. The summer
Noon upon the silent hills made all
The forests faint and left the vales athirst;
Yet, in those patriot hearts a Spartan zeal
Sustained and led them through the sultry hours
Of that immortal day their valor won.
The day was spent, and evening's grateful shade
Covered the parched earth with cooling dews,
And o'er the land a breezy incense bore,
Refreshing the tired ranks that for a space
Halted amid the Hudson's rugged steeps
To learn and do their gallant leader's will.
Anon a restless moving to and fro
Told that the hour had come, and the two columns,
Formed for battle, advanced upon the foe.
With muskets empty and with bayonets fixed,
Silently they moved, unheeding aught
That might arise to bar the way to victory.
At midnight 'neath the fortress walls they stood,
Undaunted by the rising tide that covered
All the marshy plain. Upon the fort
The watchful sentinel, pacing his quiet round,
Heard naught but the plashing tide upon the shore,
Till on the stillness fell a strange alarm

As through the palisades the patriots broke,
Making a breach for the ranks of liberty.
A cry of terror from the startled sentinels
Echoed their fear upon the midnight air,
And roused the sleeping forces from their dreams
Within the silent fort. "The foe! they come!
They come!" was loudly shouted, and the call to arms
Mingled with the din of hurrying feet now entering
Right and left under the fire of cannon.
Shot and shell filled all the night with war's
Dread sounds. "On to the fort! my brave men,
On to the fort!" rang out in clarion notes
From the lips of noble Wayne, cheering his men
To victory. Into the fort they swept, conquering
Without a shot the enemy that poured relentless
Fire into their midst. But in the flush
Of triumph the gallant General, wounded by
A random shot, fell bleeding to the earth.
His faithful followers, obedient to his faint
Command, now raised and bore him to the column's
        front,
Where by his presence he might cheer and aid.
Victor and vanquished, side by side they stood,
And the deafening shout that rent the air told
Of the patriots' glory. And they who fought and bled
Their altars to defend from hand of alien

Foe, won more than soldiers' guerdon in the
Light of bravery, humanity and a nation's pride.
The years have long since laid to sleep the hero
Whose name and deeds shall live in every heart
That throbs beneath our sky of freedom, and
The generations yet to be shall learn
To reverence, with a nation's love, the noble
Name of Wayne.

POEMS FOR LITTLE ONES.

LITTLE ELSIE TO THE FLOWERS.

Daisies, do the flowers know
  When to go to sleep?
Do they ever weary
  With the watch they keep?
Do they know who loves them,
  Do they ever sigh,
If no one is sorry
  When the roses die?

I am sure the primrose sweet
  Smiles and tries to nod:
So the purple aster
  And the golden-rod,
When I step so lightly
  In among their leaves:
If I crush a crocus,
  Pretty violet grieves.

So I think the flowers know,
  Just like me, the way
How to shut their pretty eyes
  At the close of day;

And, like me, they'd sorrow
  If no one were nigh
To watch them through their sleeping,
  Or love them when they die.

A TRUE STORY OF THE LITTLE DAUPHIN
OF FRANCE.

Long years ago, when kings and queens
  Ruled the proud court of France,
And loyal vassals bowed the knee
  Before their monarch's glance;
When wisdom, with her scepter bright,
  Spread quiet through the realm,
Monarch nor vassal dreamed of aught
  Their peace to overwhelm,
Till fell the curse of discontent
  Amid the lowly train,
And from a murmur of unrest
  Broke forth the wail of pain.
The darkest era France e'er knew
  Stamped with a crimson shame
The glory of her royalty,
  The honor of her name,
With riot and rebellion
  The world can ne'er forget.

When ruled King Louis and his queen,
  Fair Marie Antoinette,
Sovereign and subject shared alike
  The ignominious death
Who dared support the tottering throne
  By word, or act, or breath.
And ere the wrath of that fierce time
  Its vengeance had allayed,
The blood of nobles flowed in streams
  And dyed the hands that preyed.
Nor stopped they in their loathsome task,
  Nor stayed the carnage wild,
Till king and queen were sacrificed
  And the name of France defiled.
Their little son, the fair child-prince,
  Torn from love's warmest clasp,
Was placed within the keeping of
  A servile creature's grasp,
Whose chief delight, from day to day,
  Was teaching grossest sin,
And striving from the path of right
  The little prince to win.
Who, often tempted, oft did yield,
  Yet oft the tempter spurned,
For the spirit of the noble boy
  With the fire of right still burned.
And when one day the tempter's cup
  To the captive's lips was held,

Wearied with the sense of shame,
  The little heart rebelled.
The princely boy stood proudly up,
  As under seraph's wing,
And said, "I *can not* do it,
  I was born to be a king!"

And so, dear children, each of you,
  Like the little prince, may claim
The honor of a noble act,
  The heritage of fame.
If each, like him, will bravely look
  Temptation face to face,
And say, "I can not do it,"
  You may wear a prince's grace.

THE MOUSE AND THE BEE.

A mouse and a bee were discussing one day,
In a very unamiable sort of a way,
The virtues of each in his own estimation,
Of animal beauty and insect creation.
The sunshine swept in through the wide open door,
Where the disputants sat on the warm oaken floor
Of the cosy old barn, where the horse and the cow
Had fed side by side from the sweet-scented mow,

And ne'er had a thought that could lead to dissension,
And utterly scorned the disgrace of contention.
But the two tiny friends, as they sat in the sun,
Continued to talk as at first they begun:
They prated of merits that each one possessed,
And *pride* was the lever in each little breast.
"I have been," said the bee, "over mountain and vale,
I have sailed on the breeze and ridden the gale;
I have traversed the plain where the wild flowers blow,
And have lain in the blush of the rose's deep glow;
The sweets I have tasted of each little flower
That blows by the brook in sunshine and shower;
And the sights I have seen would *astonish* you so,
You would wonder and grieve you were made so low.
Just think of the honor that's granted to bees,
Of going on wings wherever they please,
While you must sit moping the live-long day,
And at most can do nothing but skip and play."
The shy little mouse was sadly confused,
As the bee smiled contempt and looked much amused,
While he waited to hear what the mouse had to say
Before spreading his wings to fly away.
"I've no doubt," said the mouse, "with the aid of your wings
You have been where you've seen most wonderful things;
But consider the privilege of being a mouse,
And living at will in a barn or a house.
While the summer time lasts I always stay here,
But hide in the house as the winter draws near,

Where I feed on the dainties that come from the table,
Never heard of in hives nor found in a stable;
And then, only think how much I must know
Of the great busy world as it moves to and fro;
For I listen to all that is talked of or read,
And of course I remember the most that is said;
While you, in your hive, can do nothing more
Than devour through the winter your whole summer's store.
Without any use for your fine pair of wings,
You must live like the wasps and such stupid things."
"You're very conceited, my friend," said the bee,
"And the sauciest mouse one might wish to see;
I will fly to the hive and report to our queen
What a miserable, impudent creature I've seen."
A pigeon, in passing, had heard the dispute,
And caught up the bee with a sudden salute,
Of "What a fine morsel, I'm really in luck,
You might have been found by a turkey or duck."
So saying, he swallowed the vain little bee,
And quickly flew off to the top of a tree.
In the meantime the old tabby cat had sneaked in
And sprang for the mouse, who ran for the bin.
But, alas! all in vain, he had lingered too late,
And at once fell a prey to a most cruel fate.

MORAL.

Had these vain little creatures been doing their duty,
Instead of disputing of virtues and beauty,

They might have been happy, each in his way,
And blessed the glad earth for many a day.
Thus the world, in its blindness, oft misses the light
That falls on the pathway of those who do right,
And gropes in the darkness of folly and sin,
Leading far from the track where the sunshine creeps in.

JACK'S NEW YEAR.

It's New Year's day to-morrow, and I've lots of things
    to do;
I must carry that sled to Ben, and the skates to his
    brother Lou;
And I promised to build a snow-fort for Burnie under the
    hill—
The factory boy that lost his arm a year ago in the
    mill.

So you see there's lots on my mind, and I'm willing to do
    it, too,
But, somehow, it don't seem the same this year that it
    used to do.
For I used to be ever so anxious for Christmas and New
    Year's fun,
For the jolliest of all the seasons that comes when the
    summer is done.

I remember I always was wishing, from January till May,
And from May around to December, and from then to
  New Year's day,
For the visit of dear old "Santy," with his sleigh and
  tiny reindeer;
But to-night, 'though I'm sure he's coming, I'm sorry to
  know he's near.

I wonder what is the matter? It must be I've done something wrong,
Or the day wouldn't lose its sunshine, and the music go
  out of my song;
For I've whistled and sung till I'm tired, and thought of
  the fun with the boys;
But something, that's just like a shadow, seems hiding
  the New Year's joys.

The fellows all like me, I'm sure, and *I* like all of *them*
  except one,
But I *hate* him, and *never*, no *never*, will I speak to him
  under the sun,
For he struck me, and called me a coward because I
  wouldn't strike back;
And I never will do him a kindness as long as my name
  is Jack.

But somehow I'm rather uneasy. I *wish* I had spoken
  last night,

When he stopped and said he was "sorry," but, of course
    I thought *I* was right,
As I turned from the gate without speaking and left the
    poor fellow outside,
But I had the *awfulest* feeling, and *almost* could have
    cried.

There's only one way to fix it. *I* must, now, go over to
    him,
Though I said I *never* would do it, but then, I always
    liked Jim,
So I'll just go to-night and tell him I shall lose all the
    New Year's joys
If I start on the New Year hating any one of the boys.

MISCHIEF.

How do you think I look
  In grandma's cap and gown,
Sitting so prim in her rocking-chair
  With the knitting she's just laid down?

I found it so still as I peeped
  Through the crack of the open door,
I thought, "Now *she's* out, *I'll* just step *in*
  And stay a minute, no more,

And try on that funny old dress
  She keeps wrapped up in a cloth,
All scented with lavender, clover and mint,
  She says is "to keep out the moth."

The dress is too long, as you see,
  There's *ever* so much on the floor,
And the cap's very large for such a small head,
  And the "specs" make the needles look *more*.

But I *guess* I can take a few stitches,
  If I look far over the rim;
Grandma herself couldn't make it look better,
  Nor draw in the edges so trim.

But mercy! She's coming! How hateful;
  I've dropped every stitch in that row,
And I've stepped on her gown and rumpled her cap,
  And *ruined* her knitting, I know.

I *wish* I had stayed down stairs,
  Playing school with Bessie and Ben,
But if grandma will only forgive me *this once*
  I *never* will meddle again.

THE LILY FAIRY.

There lived in far-off Normandy,
  Across the sunny sea,
A grandam old and little maid,
  As fair as child could be.

Florette, her name, with golden hair
  And eyes of azure hue,
That seemed reflecting from their depths
  The skies of Norman blue.

Beside a mountain stream their cot
  Lay nestled in the vale,
And at their fireside oft was heard
  A wondrous fairy tale,

Of how an elfin king, that ruled
  The fairy realm of old,
Unto an elfin witch's power
  A fairy princess sold,

Who, for a weary space of years,
  Within a lily bell
Should lie imprisoned in its heart,
  Till o'er the mystic spell

A human hand should lift the wand
  And let the sunshine in,
And from the flower prison-cell
  The fairy princess win.

The little maid had pondered oft
  With grief the fairy's doom,
And searched in vain the fields and woods
  To find the flower-tomb.

And so the days wore on apace,
  Till spring and summer faded,
And autumn smiled o'er all the land
  With gold and purple shaded.

When through the fields one shining morn
  The little maid went singing,
To fetch the water from the spring,
  She heard a distant ringing.

She paused, then through the dewy flowers
  With haste she sped along,
And as she neared the bubbling spring
  The ringing seemed a song

Which grew to words, as close she pressed
  Beside the crystal fountain,
Where in among the flowers lay hid
  The fairy of the mountain.

"Oh! haste thee, haste thee, pretty maid;
  Release me, or I die;
A hundred years I've lain, and still
  A hundred more must lie,

Unless from out my prison cell
  Some kindly hand shall free me;
Pray, let the sunshine in, Florette,
  Push back the leaves and see me."

Florette, amazed to hear her name,
  With trembling haste obeyed,
When, lo! A lily-bell sprang up
  Before the wondering maid.

The waxen petals opened wide
  As in the sunshine drifted,
And from the enchanted flower-cell
  The fairy form was lifted.

A tiny form with azure wings
  And robe of rainbow dyes,
Held forth a crown of lilies fair
  Before the childish eyes.

"This crown of shining flowers, child,"
  The fairy softly said,
"Is fashioned from the gems I love
  To place upon your head,

"In token of a fairy pledge
  To keep your feet from straying,
To light your path through storm and shine,
  At labor, or at playing:

"And when your deeds are wrought with love,
  These lilies shall grow fairer,
A shining crown upon your brow,
  A glory to the wearer."

And so it proved. As years sped on
  Kind acts brought golden treasure,
With grace and beauty, light and love,
  O'erflowed Florette's life measure.

And how, you ask, could crown of flowers
  Bring grace and love and beauty?
Good deeds were written in her life:
  She simply did her duty.

THE SPIDER AND THE FLY.

MODERN.

Have you heard the story, children,
  Of the spider and the fly;
Of how a cruel monster,
  With a wicked, flattering lie,

Inveigled to his "parlor"
  Up a mythic winding stair,
The silly little insect,
  And dined upon her there?

If not, then listen closely
  To the plan the spider laid
To secure his little victim
  With a scheme so neatly made.
Close to the spider's parlor,
  One sunny summer's day,
The pretty fly came buzzing,
  When she heard the spider say:

"Good morrow, little stranger,
  Have you journeyed far," said he.
"Just step into my parlor,
  'Tis the prettiest one might see;
Up this curious winding ladder,
  Or I *should* say winding stair,
Just follow and I'll lead you
  Where I keep my treasures rare.

"You're looking very weary,
  I *wish* you'd rest awhile;
Do dine with me, you're welcome,"
  Then turned aside to smile,

"And though I've never told it,
  You can not fail to see
How you're lovely face has won me;
  Ah, you're surely meant for me."

But the fly, suspecting mischief,
  Said, "I thank you, gentle sir;
I have hardly time to tarry *now*,
  My visit I'll defer
Till a more *convenient* morning,
  When, *perhaps*, I may drop in,
Just to look upon those treasures
  You say you have within."

The spider, nothing daunted,
  Said "Good morning" to his guest,
And added: "When you come again,
  Be sure to stop and rest."
Then to his "pretty parlor,"
  Hungry back he ran with speed,
Quite well assured his dainty guest
  Would soon supply his need.

His web he readjusted
  With a netting extra strong;
Then hastened to his doorway,
  With a most seductive song.

And sang: "Come hither, pretty fly,
  I long to see your face
And gaze into your diamond eyes,
  And view your form of grace.

"With your handsome gauzy wings,
  And robe of rainbow dyes,
You are counted very comely,
  Most clever, too, and wise.
If you doubt it, you have only
  To step in and view yourself
In a mirror at your service,
  Just upon my parlor shelf."

Alas! the silly insect,
  Caught by the wily song,
Thinking only of her beauty,
  Without a fear of wrong,
Soon returned to view the "parlor,"
  With its boasted "treasures rare,"
And to gaze upon her features
  In the little mirror there.

The spider watched her coming,
  And hid within his den.
She labored up his "winding stair,"
  But ne'er came down again,

And all too late she learned the truth,
  That wisdom ne'er is found,
In listening to a tempter's song,
  Where flattering words abound.

PUSHED OUT OF THE NEST.

Oh dear! How I shiver, although it is May!
  But they tell me that all's for the best,
Yet I wonder what father and mother *can* mean
  By pushing me out of the nest!

Since the day we came out of some tiny blue shells,
  In our soft little nest on the tree,
They've fed us with morsels of bugs and worms,
  My two little brothers and me.

But to-day when they fed us our breakfast of bugs,
  Which they found in the field of clover,
They coaxed me up to the edge of the nest.
  Then quietly pushed me over!

What's that in the grass? A cat, as I live!
  Dear me! how I wish I could fly!
But my wings are too small and my body so large,
  And the trees seem so very high!

But he's coming this way! He's seen me, I'm sure!
  I *must* try my wings at least!
There! really, I'm safe on the top of this bush,
  And the cat's cheated out of a feast!

Well, flying *is* easy, if one only tries,
  But one never learns in the nest;
So, whenever pushed out by the old birds, be sure
  You will soon learn what's for the best.

CHRISTMAS CAROL.

Hail, holy morn!
  The advent of our King!
To Christ the Savior born
  All glory bring!
Chant the anthem's heavenly strain,
Sung of old on Bethlehem's plain,
  Glory in the highest sing,
    Glory! Glory! Glory!

Peace on earth proclaim,
  And good-will to men!
Hail the Princely Name,
  Chant His praise again!

Render now Thy will be done,
Bow before the Holy One!
Glory ever to the same,
Glory! Glory! Glory!

Ye weary, loosed from sin,
No longer prostrate lie!
Glad tidings enter in
From heralds of the sky!
Earth's redeemed! With seraphs sing
Hallelujahs to our King!
Glory be to God on high.
Glory! Glory! Glory!

DRAMA FOR LITTLE ONES.

LOVE'S VICTORY.

DRAMATIS PERSONÆ:

Prince Rudolph, of Castle Offenstein.
Lady Constance, of Castle Waldenbeck.
Otto, Page to the Prince.
Zephyr, the Fairy Godmother, who presided at Lady Constance's birth.

SCENE I—In Waldenbeck Wood.
SCENE II—Chapel in the Wood.
SCENE III—The ball at Castle Offenstein.

Finale—Fairy Ballet.

The Drama to be used as a final production in a parlor entertainment, to consist of recitations, tableaux, music and charades, *ad libitum*. A century's feud broken by the marriage of Prince Rudolph to Lady Constance.

Page Otto—

'Tis late, my Lord, why linger in this wood?
Surely from waiting cometh nothing good.

Prince Rudolph—

'Tis never late while waiting for one's Love!
Have patience, Page of mine, all things above.

Page Otto—

    And yet the hour is past, the tryst unkept,
    And all the bounds of patience overstepped.

Prince Rudolph—

    Fear not, good Otto, for by yonder moon
    I'll wage my Lady Constance cometh soon.

Page Otto—

    The midnight hour has tolled, the moon dips low:
    Methinks the Lady Constance rideth slow.

Prince Rudolph—

    She rideth near, in sooth, the saints are good!
    E'en now I hear her near the chapel wood.

Page Otto—

    'Tis true, my Lord; no longer may you wait;
    Love conquers time, though oft he conquers late.

    Enter from forest path Lady Constance, alone.

Lady Constance—

    Ah, Rudolph! Patient lover! I am here at last,
    Though many dangers 'round my path were cast.

Prince Rudolph—

    But safe at last, and free from baneful charm;
    We only wait fair Zephyr to shield us from all harm.

Zephyr—

    No longer wait. Behold me at your side!
    What wouldst thou, Prince, my lady for a bride?

Prince Rudolph—

> My Lady Constance and her constant love,
> A guerdon, Fairy, all other gifts above!

Zephyr—

> The priest is waiting in the old Chapelle;
> Will wed ye ere the new day's matin bell.

Prince Rudolph—

> A blessing, Fairy, we would crave of thee,
> At midnight here within the forest free.

Zephyr's Blessing—

> The towers of Waldenbeck for thee shall shine,
> The Flower of Waldenbeck, my Lord, is thine.

Prince Rudolph, Lady Constance and Page Otto sing thanks to Zephyr.

All singing—

> Thanks to thee, Fay, for thy gentle grace!
> Long may ye reign in the greenwood place!
> Queen may ye reign in the greenwood bowers!
> Hover and guard over Waldenbeck Towers!

IMPROMPTU LINES.

TO * * *

I know not how the coming days shall waken,
  Nor if to them their light will constant be;
I only know that when your light is taken,
  It will be darkness till you dawn on me.

OMNE TEMPUS.

What shall I write, sweet friend,
That Time shall not amend,
    Nor years distort?
The Gold of life be yours,
The love that best endures
    Through storms to port!

DAVIS'S MILL.

God sent the sunshine, fairest gift,
  To glad the heart of Nature,
But left the gift to gladden life
  With one fair human creature.

July 30, 1884.

THY PRESENCE.

There is no day without thee,
  There is no night complete;
The glory of thy presence
  Makes all things fair and sweet.

YOU.

Write you "something sweet." Love,
  "I've nothing else to do"?
All the sweet in life, Love,
  I write in writing "You."

ST. AGNES EVE.

I kissed you, Dear, in dreams
  On sweet St. Agnes Eve,
And the night held rosy beams,
  Such as fays from sunlight weave.

AUGUST AFTERNOON.

The shadows lengthen, Oh, how sweet!
The glories deepen, Oh, how meet
  For such a day!

All that a life may hold
These golden hours enfold,
  Now dying at our feet.

FROM ME TO THEE.

In love's language truly told,
  Read within the story old,
Brief and quaint the tale will be;
  Read and find "From *me* to *thee*."

ANON.

Life's music ever fails us
  Till its saddest strains are sung;
'Tis only out of sorrow
  All the sweetest notes are wrung.

CHRISTMAS VERSES.

TO ——.

I send with the flowers
  This Christmas morn
Love's greeting warm and true,
With a blessing, Dear, that will last for aye,
When the flowers and words have faded away,
  And my heart has no more to do.

TO A. X.

Open your heart to a little guest,
  Sent to greet you this Christmas day,
In love's garment gaily drest;
  He will whisper what I say.
With the chimes across the snow
Peace and love to you will flow.

TO * * *

Accept my love this Christmas day;
It will tell you all that the year could say
Of a love that will last forever and aye,

Beyond life's night and morning,
Beyond the shadow of earthly bound,
Where the light of all Christmas-tides is found.
The celestial land adorning.

TO ——

No new love words can I say,
Dear One, on this Christmas day;
No new music can I bring
With the words my heart will bring;
But to words and music made,
On love's altar for thee laid,
Let me, to enrich the rest.
To "I love thee" add "the best."

AUTOGRAPH SCRAPS.

TO S. M.

In after years, when looking back
   Through memory's misty veil,
Your weary heart shall idly count
   The shadows dim and pale,

And, counting, call again the friends
   Your sunny girlhood knew;
Let memory place me in the rank
   Among the tried and true.

TO A. M. W.

A *bal masque* is life on a very grand scale,
   And the maskers are thronging its portals;
Some laugh as they enter, and some stop to sigh,
   And some are the saddest of mortals.

Now try to be gay, and laugh with the throng,
   Reach alway and ever for roses,
And if hurt by the thorns, a balm you will find,
   In a sweetness each petal discloses.

TO C. S.

My name for this casket of flowers,
  I assure you, is worthless indeed;
You ask for a rose, but instead,
  Behold, you have naught but a " *Weed*."

TO ALICE A.

Carefully ponder the truth I give,
  With full permission to lend:
There's nothing on earth so hard to find
  As a true and faithful friend.

TO LOUIE W.

In your heart's corridor,
  Ringing love's whisper,
Carry my singing
  Down to life's vesper.

TO C. H.

My dear little girl, when you grow to a woman,
  And read o'er the wishes now written for you,
May your heart in its search for a love yet unspoken,
  Find all it requires to banish life's "rue."

May the links of love's forging be left in your keeping,
  And held still unbroken by time in its flight,
And may all that can bless and brighten life's pathway
  Be yours, little girl. till the coming of night.

TO L. R.

The violet blooms by the singing brook,
  And sheds its sweets for a day;
The primrose buds in the wayside nook,
  Then blushing fades away.

So I will not bring to wear on your heart
  The flower so soon forgot,
But one that shall last till life shall cease,
  The treasured forget-me-not.

TO H. E. S.

Whenever you wander to this little spot,
  The very last one in the book,
Look close and the floweret forget-me-not
  You'll find in this little nook.

TO N. S.

Along the path of life you tread,
  Though thorns may wound your feet,
    In the hedges low
    The roses blow,
  A healing balm of sweet.

TO F. S.

'Tis better to have held the roses,
　Though the hand that held them bled,
Than never to have known their sweetness
　Ere their fragrance all had fled.

Better far to pluck the lilies,
　Rocking on their tiny stems,
Than to let them droop and wither,
　Ruined, wasted diadems.

Better 'tis to know the morning,
　Even though the shadows fall,
Than forever dwell in darkness,
　And enjoy no rays at all.

So grieve not if hurt by roses,
　Mourn not for the lilies slain,
Morning comes and brings its healing
　And restores all sweets again.

ACROSTICS.

GARFIELD.

Great-hearted hero! A country's pride!
  All nations mourn the quenching of his light;
Round the vast globe the echoes still abide;
  Fond hearts are mourning still a nation's blight.
Into the "Shadow-Land," with pilgrim-shoon,
  Entered the martyr-chief, life's battle o'er;
Leaving earth's mystery for the heavenly rune,
  Dawn found him mid the glories of the better shore.

NEAL.

Not the seraphs above in that dreamland of glory,
  Ever sing without love in that region of bliss.
All the choristers kneeling chant low the sweet story,
  Love reigns in that realm as it rules over this.

MAY.

May all the blessings life can hold
Around thy pathway closely fold, and
Yield love's magic gifts of gold.

BIRTHDAY VERSES.

TO ——

Accept these violets, Dear:
  Their muteness may serve so well
To tell you all in their quiet way
  What my heart is too far to tell.

And may the sweets they breathe
  Pervade the coming years,
And may each dawn be crowned with love,
  Each close undimmed by tears.

TO C. C. H.

Fair friend. I wish thee fair
  In all that life may send:
Fond hearts thine own to wear,
Life's years untouched by care,
  Be thine till life shall end.

IN MEMORIAM.

Oh, silvery tones now vanished,
  Borne down the waste to me,
Through all life's day will echo,
  "My faith looks up to Thee."

Our trembling lips will falter,
  Our tears we can not hide;
Our empty hearts will weary,
  Calling till eventide.

All through the days unlighted,
  And through the years to be,
Across the shadowed silence,
  Our hearts will reach to Thee;

And passionately calling,
  Will yearn once more to hear
Thy fond voice softly whisper,
  Thy spirit draw anear.

And far adown the silence,
  Across life's boundless sea,
Will float for aye the murmur:
  "My faith looks up to Thee."

Ah! that our warm earth-kisses,
  Close pressed to lips so mute,
Might wake again life's music
  From out the silent lute,

To teach us in our weeping,
  Low on the bended knee,
With trusting hearts to murmur:
  "My faith looks up to Thee."

Greenwich, Conn., December 11, 1878.